Originally published as *Ella het swingende eendje* in Belgium and the Netherlands by Clavis Uitgeverij, 2018
English translation from the Dutch by Clavis Publishing Inc., New York

Visit us on the Web at www.clavis-publishing.com.

Ella the Swinging Duck written by Suzan Overmeer and illustrated by Myriam Berenschot

ISBN 978-1-60537-498-7 (hardcover edition)
ISBN 978-1-60537-517-5 (softcover edition)

This book was printed in January 2020 at Nikara, M. R. Štefánika 858/25, 963 01 Krupina, Slovakia.

First Edition
10 9 8 7 6 5 4 3 2 1

Written by Suzan Overmeer
Illustrated by Myriam Berenschot

Ella
the
Swinging
Duck

Clavis

NEW YORK

Mildred and Maury Duck liked everything just so.
They were the most distinguished ducks in the land.
They ate their duckweed with a knife and fork,
and afterward, cleaned their bills with napkins.
When they had something to say, they quacked politely.

One day, Mildred Duck laid seven eggs in her fancy nest.

A few weeks later the ducklings were born.
The first six quietly stepped out of their eggs.
Mildred gave them elegant names.
She called them Wolfgang, Ludwig, Hildegard,
Johan-Sebastian, Clara-Belle, and Amadeus.

From the last egg rolled a little girl duckling.
She fell on her bill and quacked hello loudly.

Mildred looked at her and said: "I will call you *Ella*."

Ella was different from her brothers and sisters.
She always waddled out of the line.
She made up her own songs to sing.
She was loud and silly.

Mildred hoped that Ella would be
more serious when she grew up.

Ella's brothers and sisters thought **Ella** was strange.
"Ella-umbrella!" called Hildegard.
"You are such a silly duck!" teased Johan-Sebastian.

Ella was sad. She went off searching
for someone to sing and swing with.

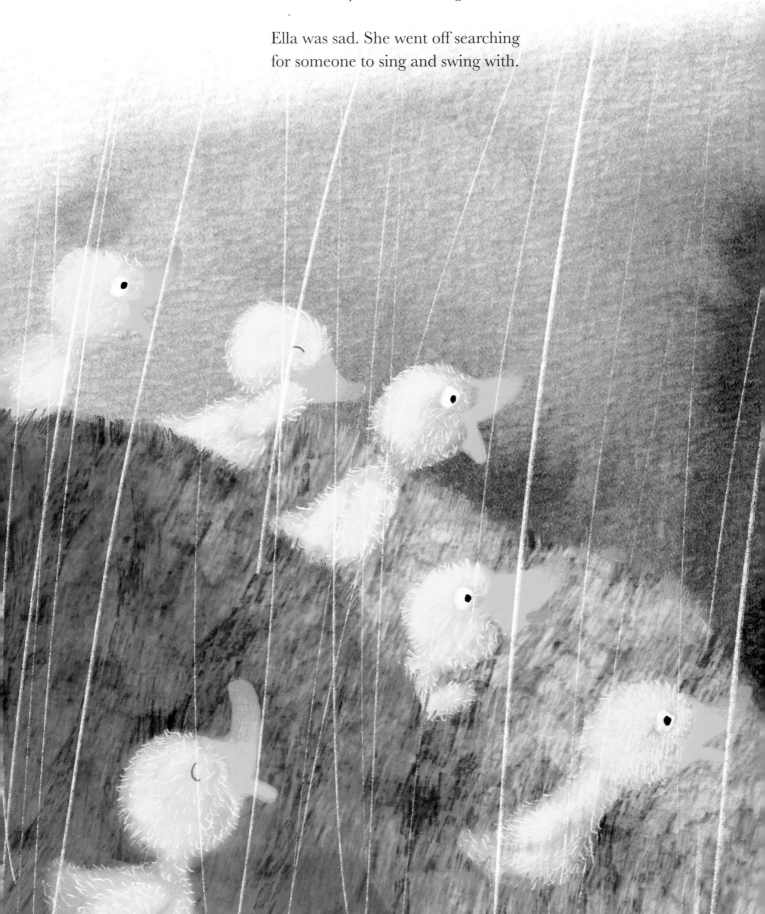

Suddenly **Ella** heard a sound.
The little duck swam toward it and saw a dove
on a bridge. "**Coo, coo!**" the dove sang.
Ella couldn't wait to join in!
"**Doobee doo daaa,**" she sang along.

"**Stop!**" cried the dove.
"What are you doing?"
"I'm *Ella*. I want to make music with you,"
she said with a small voice.
"I only sing alone," said the dove. "Off you go!"
Ella swam away sadly.

After a while, *Ella* heard singing again and she swam toward the sound.
She saw a group of frogs singing on a lily pad.
"**Croak, croak, crooaak!**" the frogs sang.
"I'll join in!" Ella cheered.
"**Doobee doo dee,**" Ella chattered happily.

"**Hey!**" said the big frog.
"Who are you? What are you doing?"
Ella immediately stopped singing. "My name is Ella.
I'd like to make music with you," she said with a small voice.
"We are the Frogs Choir," the frog bellowed. "You can't join us! Now go!"
Ella swam away again.

Ella was lonely. She just wanted someone to sing with.
"Doo daa dee," she sang.
Suddenly she heard a sound.
"Doo daa dee . . ."
Ella was startled. Who was it?

Then Ella noticed a beak peeking through the flowers.
"Are you singing along, la la long?" she sang.
"Yes, I'm singing along, la la long!" someone giggled.
"Who are you?" Ella asked curiously.
For a moment nothing happened, but then
a little swan came into view.

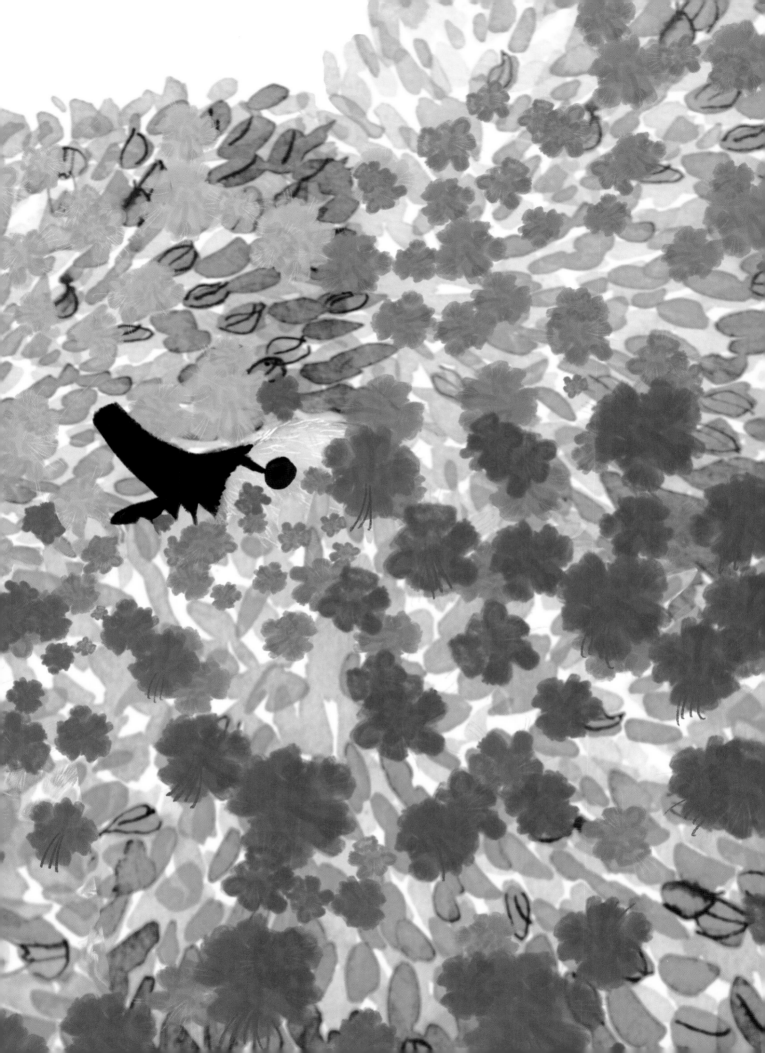

The swan was young and gray and all alone.
"I'm DIZZY," he said. "Everybody teases me
because I like to blast with my bill."
"Toot toot toot taa toot!" DIZZY sang.
Ella beamed. "I like your blast!"

Ella and DIZZY became fast friends.
They made up their own songs and sang all day long.
Soon, all the animals in the wood were dancing and swinging to the beat.

Ella was almost happy. The only thing that was missing
was her family. So she decided to head home.
And she brought her new friend with her . . .

The Duck family was surprised by the two musical friends!
Amadeus started to tap his wings to the beat.
Ludwig and Wolfgang hummed along softly, and soon all the brothers
and sisters were singing along: "**Quack quack doobee daa!**"

Ella was overjoyed. She had a great friend to make music with . . .
and she was home again!

Dooba da, dooba dee
I make my own melody
I like to sing
And I like to swing

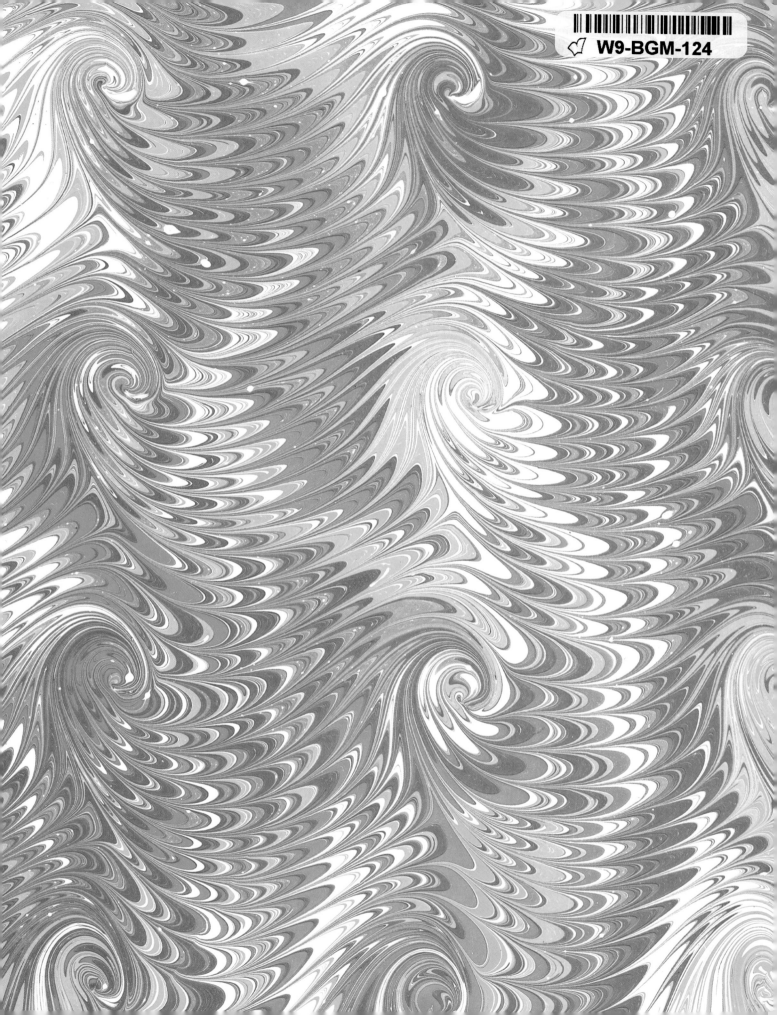

Lynnell K Schwartz

Vintage Compacts & Beauty Accessories

Lynell
Schwartz

Schiffer Publishing Ltd

77 Lower Valley Road, Atglen, PA 19310

To Hazel, Esther, and Annie,
three wonderful Aunts
who have been there all along.

And to Paige Annabelle,
the newest addition to our family.

Printed in Hong Kong

ISBN: 0-7643-0110-1

Cover Design & Book Layout by Michael William Potts

Published by Schiffer Publishing Ltd.
77 Lower Valley Road
Atglen, PA 19310
Phone: (610) 593-1777 Fax: (610) 593-2002
E-mail: schifferbk@aol.com

Please write for a free catalog.
This book may be purchased from the publisher.
Please include $2.95 for shipping.
Try your bookstore first.

We are interested in hearing from authors
with book ideas on related subjects.

Vintage Compacts & Beauty Accessories

Contents

Acknowledgments

A very special thank you to Carol Schwartz for proof-reading expertise, William Schwartz for his artistic and photographic contributions, and Walter Kitik for his all-around support.

To Eric Kitik and Jason for computer support.

Thanks to Carl Tunestam, Stephanie Novell, Sharon Hall, Michael and Gloria Kaplan, Joyce Morgan, and Rosanna Polizzotto.

My gratitude to the foremost collectors in the United States for their unwavering enthusiasm, support, and for their efforts in photographing their outstanding compact collections and sharing them with all of us, allowing us to behold a wonderful variety of vintage compacts.

Thank you to Nancy and Peter Schiffer for their support and enthusiasm for this project.

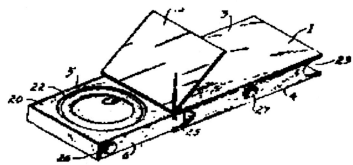

P 1,837,722

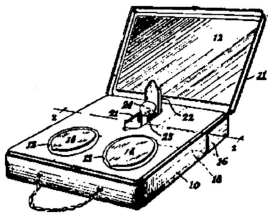

P 1,875,650

Introduction

One of my first exposures to vintage compacts came many years ago—almost by accident! I received a call from a collector that lived many states away. She was changing tastes in collecting, and wanted to sell her collection of compacts and concentrate on kitchen items. She continued to describe what type of compacts she had amassed and put a flat price on the entire bunch. Of course, I was interested. After all, I was already in the antique business.

When the box arrived, I was instantly enamored. There were two compacts with watches embedded into the design, one resembling a pocket watch, Richard Hudnuts, Evans, Elgin Americans, Elizabeth Ardens, a musical carryall with cigarette compartment that played "Smoke Gets in Your Eyes," a Bakelite bolster shaped vanity with a black tassel, and among other things, what I thought was most unusual at the time: an enameled mesh purse by Whiting and Davis with a compact incorporated into the frame.

Now, the dilemma...what do I charge for them? Each had its own distinctive personality and was unusual in its own way. There were no available books on the subject so it was impossible to simply pick up a guide to help determine value. Furthermore, I would not be keeping them, but instead, opted to sell all. So, I did what most antique dealers do. I priced them according to what I paid for them. Needless, to say, the compacts sold quickly! Most could have been sold many times if I had been lucky enough to have duplicates!

This early endeavor with compacts was a great experience. I learned which ones were most desired, and best of all, gathered "want lists" for future compact purchases, and even found purse collectors as a result of advertising the vanity purse previously mentioned. My compact business built over time and this foundation, along with research and many years of extensive antique show exhibiting, helped to pave the way to write this book and my previous book, *Vintage Purses at their Best*.

Today, many years later, I specialize in vintage compacts, purses, and costume jewelry, and it has been the most exciting adventure that I can hope to have. Each phone call and every turn at an antiques show carries the potentiality of finding the elusive collectible that's never been seen, or even heard about before. It's a challenge to find something extremely rare, research it, and place a value on it. Imagine how I felt when I found the two whimsical French figural powders shown in this book, a Parisian Henry A. La Pensee artist's palette, or when I was presented with the sardine can compact with turn key opener!

Now, great compacts are harder to find than ever. But the latest collection I acquired, all of which are shown in this book, prove that hot air balloons, castanets, Dali's birds, Schuco monkeys, and other whimsical figural and fun compacts are still out there. My only regret is a pair of rare cat compacts, which I spied at a recent antique show. One was a full figure, the other, only the face, both consisting of natural looking material made to look like short brown animal fur. Sure, they were expensive, and I hesitated. But someone else didn't. The cost of the compacts? Well...with hindsight, I should have paid the price since that was the last I've seen of those two cat compacts!

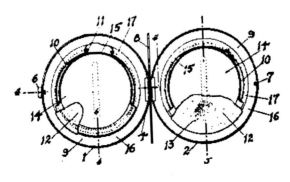

P 1,874,433

P 1,814,748

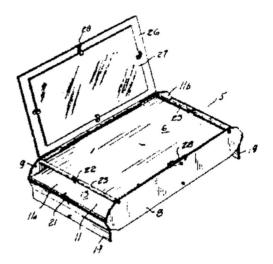

P 1,866,162

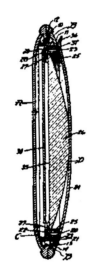

1,875,245

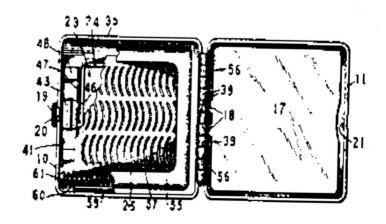

P 1,863,856

Chapter One
A History of Cosmetics

Manufacturers in the twenties and thirties took a look back at toilet goods, packages, and containers from early history through the ages as a helpful stimulus for "new" designs and a source of inspiration for ideas. Part of the reason why compacts are so clever is that the importance of revisiting the history of cosmetics was not lost among the best artists, designers, and decorators who had training studying earlier works. Ideas came from something as simple as reproducing a flower design from a rich piece of fabric from ancient China—ideal for a powder package—or as intricate as a marble Greek figure that sets the tempo for a perfume bottle.

An unusual antique box in classic Persian design that was originally a make-up container. The eleven compartments all held a beauty product that was essential to ancient feminine beauty. Manufacturers imitated it by producing different types of ensemble dressing cases and redesigned them for modern use. *The American Perfumer*.

Early in the twentieth century, powder was the choice cosmetic and was fluffed all over the face with large puffs, leaving a pale effect that covered the eyelashes and eyebrows.

Industry today looks to those in the early twentieth century to determine what techniques of marketing, manufacturing, and other approaches were successful. Studying earlier and even ancient receptacles for cosmetics and toilet goods helps to ascertain how and in what manner they can be adapted for modern use.

An example of a piece of the past that was redesigned is an unusual antique box in classic Persian motif that was originally a make-up container. It has a larger paisley shaped piece resembling a leaf in the center, set off by smaller versions all around it. All of the peculiar shaped mini boxes have lids. Each leaf is attached by a wire and lifts up. The eleven compartments all held a beauty product that was essential to ancient feminine beauty. One could have contained face powder, while another a rosy color for the cheeks, and so on. Manufacturers imitated it by producing different types of ensemble dressing cases and redesigned them for modern use.

At the turn of the century, women wore little make-up in public, especially during the day. Pinching cheeks and biting lips was virtually a woman's only available option for adding color to the face. In the teens, powder was the choice cosmetic and was fluffed all over the face with huge puffs. It left a pale effect that covered eyelashes and eyebrows.

The first sweep of metal compacts was ridiculed and nicknamed "trunks" because they were so large and awkward. They also carried the name "puff boxes," and the powder was belittled and called "concrete." The term "compact" was later introduced and the use of slip cover metal boxes was superseded by hinged containers.

Along came the twenties, and women began using mascara and eyeshadow more frequently with the appearance of Swedish-born Greta Garbo. Two major trends developed in compact design and just about everything else. One was called the Egyptian Revival period, in which the decorative subject matter used in compact making was affected by the interest brought on after the discovery of King Tutankhamen's tomb by Howard Carter in 1922. The other influence was the Art Deco period.

The Egyptian revival period began after Howard Carter discovered the tomb of a nine year old pharaoh, who, during his short reign of Egypt (about 1334 B.C.), was married to Ankhesenamun, the daughter of Nafertiti, famed to be the most beautiful woman of all time.

The ancient Egyptian custom of decorating the face with make-up was revived when the first little cardboard boxes of rouge and lipstick came cautiously on the market. Step by step, the first metal boxes were made in Europe and then painstakingly copied by American manufacturers.

The ancient Egyptian custom of decorating the face with make-up was revived when the first little cardboard boxes of rouge came cautiously on the market. Following were cardboard lipstick containers, and step by step, the first metal boxes were made in Europe and then painstakingly copied by American manufacturers.

The fashion trends of famous women like "moving picture stars" persuaded the public to tint cheeks and lips, and to intensify their eyebrows and lids. Daring women began spreading petroleum jelly on their eyelids and wore cake mascara and rouge. Eyeshadow was seldom used. Lipstick was both seldom used by some or boldly worn by others.

"Daring" women spread petroleum jelly on their eyelids and wore cake mascara and rouge in the early part of the twentieth century.

Egyptian revival red enameled compact with gilded pharaoh on lid. The powder puff is signed "Clarice Jane." 2" x 4". *From the Collection of Kay Miguez, Photograph by Miguez Photography*. $175-225.

Earrings were long with golden images of the Sphinx set to dangle from the ears. Bauble rings carved from tiger-eye and lapis were made to emulate the pharaoh, cobras, and lotus blossoms, all of which had special significance to Egyptians. Special symbols like hieroglyphics, messages of resurrection and eternal life that carried specific messages thousands of years ago, once again beckoned and were looked upon with great mystery and admiration. These important pieces of cosmetic's past were also found in Egyptian history:

In February 1923, the day the Burial Chamber was to be opened, the press and photographers from all over waited impatiently in the Egyptian sun, eager to bring news to people all over the world. Once the pharaoh's coffin was excavated from the massive enclosure of the sarcophagus and the body, encased in a solid gold inner coffin, was excavated there was no stopping the fervor that followed. Designers, compact manufacturers, and fashion experts began creating jewelry, purses, compacts, and fashion accessories to mimic the ancient artifacts and treasures recently uncovered. Soon, leaders in the fashion industry in New York, London, and Paris were designing bolts of cloth with a decided Egyptian influence.

Compacts made in the 1920s were influenced as they too were caught up in the intensity of this unique historical discovery. French celluloid compacts were pressed to recreate the images of the ruler and his followers. Gilded pharaohs with raised golden heads peered above the lids of compacts during this period of Egyptian revival. Compacts were molded from celluloid and carved from Bakelite. Metal accents depicting the young pharaoh were machined to decorate compact lids. Celluloid powder containers for the dressing table had godlike images impressed into their lids. Jewelry and other accessories were created in the form of scarabs; bracelets were made in gold and silver with plated shells of real beetles, considered to be sacred to the Egyptians.

French fabric vanity case with pharaoh's head, silk tassel, and carry cord, accentuated with glass balls. 4" x 4". *Lori Landgrebe Antiques*. $120-170.

Elgin American gilded metal compact with Egyptian design in presentation box. 3" x 3". *Lori Landgrebe Antiques*. $95-125.

From the XVIII Dynasty, a dish of alabaster in the shape of a fish or lotus, used for condiments or cosmetics, that could have provided inspiration for later use as a make-up ensemble.

Three jars from a set of Princess Sat-hathor-iunut of the XII Dynasty. They are of obsidian and mounted in gold. The cosmetic vases are part of a set of three identical containers and the kohl pot has a small round opening under the lid. In the 1930s, they were reproduced using black plastic and brass mounted caps.

Three unguent boxes or jars, the first is of the XIX Dynasty, Ramese, II (1292-1225 B.C.) and is made of ivory. On the lid appears the King's name and that of his queen, Nefretiri. There is a trace of what appears as though it might be rouge of some kind. A swivel hinge is located on one side and a raised handle to swing the cover off is found on the other. There is also a button-like projection from the dish to which perhaps a cord or loop of some other material was used to fasten down the top securely. An armadillo-like animal decorates the lid. The other two jars of the XVIII Dynasty show similar dishes and means of fastening the lid, but all work on the swivel bases and is something that modern day cosmetics have not employed for such containers. The beautiful delicate tracery of design is quite apparent and inspired designers of the twenties and thirties.

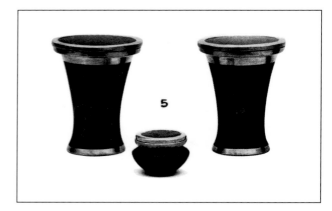

Historic Egyptian cosmetic receptacles provided inspiration and ideas for manufacturers like these three jars from a set of Princess Sat-hathor-iunut of the XII Dynasty of obsidian and mounted in gold. The cosmetic vases are part of a set of three identical containers and the kohl pot has a small round opening under the lid. In the 1930s, they were reproduced using black plastic and brass mounted caps. *The American Perfumer*, 1935.

From the XVIII Dynasty, a dish of alabaster in the shape of a fish or lotus used for condiments or cosmetics, which could have provided inspiration for later use as a make-up ensemble. *The American Perfumer*, 1935.

A palette with wells containing six colors. At the top, the palette bears the names of Amenhotep III "Nibmare Beloved of Re" and was made of ivory. It is traced to the XVIII Dynasty, and the reign of Amenhotep III. With its beauty and simplicity of design, this palette, possibly used for rouge, was reproduced in the early twentieth century.

The other strong influence to compact manufacturing in the 1920s was the Art Deco period which began with the opening of *Exposition Internationale des Arts Decoratifs et Industriels Modernes* in 1925. The Parisian exhibition promoted modern stylization with geometric shapes and vivid colors that infiltrated designs of furniture, clothing, jewelry, purses, and compacts. Fads and trends like both Egyptian Revival and the Art Deco period skyrocketed quickly and eventually waned, leaving the astute compact manufacturer searching for new ideas.

Three unguent boxes or jars. The first is of the XIX Dynasty, Ramese, II (1292-1225 B.C.) and is made of ivory. On the lid appears the king's name and that of his queen, Nefretiri. There is a trace of what appears to be rouge of some kind. The other two jars of the XVIII Dynasty show similar designs. The beautiful delicate style is quite apparent and inspired designers of the twenties and thirties. *The American Perfumer*, 1935.

With its beauty and simplicity of design, this palette, possibly used for rouge, was reproduced in the early twentieth century. At the top it bears the names of Amenhotep III "Nibmare Beloved of Re" and was made of ivory, it is traced to the XVIII Dynasty, and the reign of Amenhotep III. *The American Perfumer*, 1935.

A strong influence to compact manufacturing was the Art Deco period which began with the opening of *Exposition Internationale des Arts Decoratifs et Industriels Modernes* in Paris in 1925, prompting bold geometric shapes. 2½" x 2½". *The Curiosity Shop*. $45-65.

In the thirties, eyebrows were shaved or plucked thin and penciled in to keep up with celebrity trends. Bleach masks were used to cover suntans and discolorations of the skin and pancake make-up became the first face foundation.

At an early juncture of the manufacturer's compact production career came an important question: Do I want to make an inexpensive mass-produced product that I can sell in quantity at the five and dime or novelty stores, or do I want to create unique pieces with hand made touches that will prosper once I become established at exclusive jewelry stores? The latter was a larger investment of both time and money. Designers, enamelists, and other specialty employees who could help create uncommon compacts were just a part of the increased costs.

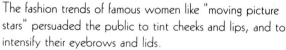
The fashion trends of famous women like "moving picture stars" persuaded the public to tint cheeks and lips, and to intensify their eyebrows and lids.

A fascinating piece of cosmetic's history is the charming five and dime store where these cosmetics were purchased inexpensively. This go-between for the mass production manufacturer and the eager consumer, was a perfect testing ground for new ideas in compacts, make-up, and other items. Many compacts found today came from these delightful and historic places.

PAN-CAKE MAKE-UP

It is a new kind of make-up, originated by *Max Factor Hollywood*, that actually seems to create a new complexion.

It makes the skin look soft and smooth as velvet. It helps conceal every tiny complexion fault. It stays on for hours without re-powdering.

First introduced in Technicolor pictures, Pan-Cake Make-Up is Hollywood's new secret of a "glamour complexion."

ROSALIND RUSSELL
Metro-Goldwyn-Mayer

Pancake make-up became the first foundation in the 1930s. Max Factor s pancake make-up is endorsed by Rosalind Russell in this advertisement. *The New Art of Make-Up*, 1940.

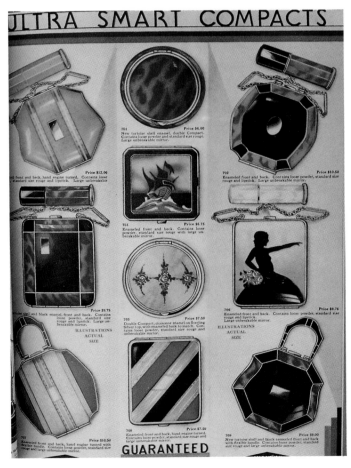

Some Art Deco inspired compacts offered in 1932 by The Marathon Company. *Deutsch and Marks catalog.*

Volume selling in the five and dime store is where the profit of the manufacturer was earned. It was a place not too pretentious for the kind hearted day laborer buying "that pretty nail shine" for his daughter, yet fascinating to the most sophisticated flapper trying out new beauty tricks. The store held a steady business, where day in and out, the cosmetic counter was rarely free from customers. Seventeen to twenty at a time was not unusual.

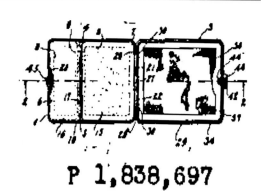

P 1,838,697

A glimpse inside the five and dime store of the 1930s where compacts and cosmetics were sold in volume. *The American Perfumer*, 1934.

Attractive cosmetic window displays like these were on display in the early 1930s. *The American Perfumer*, 1932.

The average customer for the five and dime store, like F.W. Woolworth Company or Kresge, from a typical Mid-Western city such as Des Moines, Iowa, was studied in 1933. The city was feeling the depression, yet was no more severely hit than the ordinary city. The Kresge store was observed at various times of the day on different days. Long before computer technology was available to determine which products are selling the most successfully, the observer in the thirties had to inconspicuously sidle along beside each prospective customer when purchasing cosmetics and observe how the selection was made. The goal was to get genuine customer reaction to report back to the manufacturer of the product.

The dime store would devote an entire window display to cosmetics. Each item would be featured either with its carton or mounted on an attractive card. The center of the window would be given over to eye catching objects like the new bottles and boxes of Chamberlain Hand Lotion, Campana's Italian Balm, and Terri Cosmetic's powder boxes, to name a few. Holiday gift boxes that included compacts, powders, perfumes, creams, and other toiletries were popular store front items. It was important for manufacturers to have colorful boxes and pretty compact designs not only to induce the customer's purchase, but the attractiveness of a bottle and the striking color scheme of its carton also had to be a temptation that would be hard to resist for the window designer.

The study found that the typical customer at the five and ten, what was termed as the "sable coat" trade, was using the department as a means of buying guest room sizes of cosmetics to be used for week-end guests and then thrown away. The "seal coat" customer had also become a steady, come-back source of business. The majority of the customers were young matrons of the upper middle classes whose scheme of life included a wide range of toilet goods, but whose budget demanded smaller expenditures, and young girls who wanted everything from eye lash curler to wave set. The observer watched groups come up to the counter: two high school girls eagerly studying each new item, a man buying face powder, a woman making a choice of nail enamel. After observing hundreds of sales, there were two important conclusions: the amount of sales resistance was small, yet the clientele for the greatest part was an educated one, with set standards of what they wanted.

Like people at a big bargain sale, they were eager to find something they could like, and needed no persuasion. Sales averaged about fifteen cents per customer. They had come ready to buy and wanted to be convinced, but whose products they bought depended on many things.

Customer appeal was induced by the familiar name. National radio advertising with Wayne King helped to encourage purchases of Lady Esther powders and creams. The attractive coral and blue cream jar and the recognition factor helped to put these products in the lead during the span of the survey. Not all cartons had explicit directions, but the ones that did held a decided advantage in attracting attention and then in retaining interest sufficiently enough to make a sale.

Women began using mascara and eyeshadow more frequently with the appearance of Swedish-born Greta Garbo.

"Is this new, is it safe?" were some of the queries overheard. Doubts and timidity about trying new products were squelched when the stamp of the Good Housekeeping Institute was observed. Another determining factor was a packaging feature for purse convenience and a growing preference for cosmetics in pencil form. For lip rouge, deodorant, nail white, eye shadow, and a long list of toilet requisites, the observer saw hesitation before the familiar forms, and then the customer would choose the pencil and slip it into their purse. Smaller packages also took preference in the case of perfume and lipstick, as though a small quantity was assurance that the product was very good. In face powder, the public wanted to see the shade, and smell the perfume of the powder. Customers would lift the lid, smell it, and then determine the tint they wanted. When not being purchased as a gift, and the user herself was buying it, she would often buy the compact that could be opened and examined, or a cardboard powder box that had a transparent drum cover, rather than be content with just the name of the shade.

Another important consideration in determining whose product the customer would purchase was the power of the salesperson to offer advice, information, and sway opinion. A firm that sent a letter, sample, or cosmetic chart to the department head telling the virtues of the product found the salesperson more prepared to answer questions and thus more inclined to make a sale.

But whether at an exclusive shop or discount store, manufactured from metal, plastic, or some other material, classic simplicity and beauty on the outside, combined with the accuracy of mechanical skill on the inside, was usually the winning combination.

Many novelty and figural compacts were sold in five and dime stores like Woolworth and Kresge. *The American Perfumer*, 1934.

Vanity case design drawing, by an artist working for Bliss/Napier in the early twentieth century. *The Napier Company archives*.

Still, quite a few manufacturers went to the expense of making special cases that were unique in either construction or decoration. They undertook private dies, protected them by patents, and the finished products were not available in stock numbers. Nevertheless, the advancement of compacts went spiralling forward when intermediate sized manufacturers, who weren't in a position to chance the high cost of tools to create entirely unique compacts, discovered an alternate solution. By taking well designed, standard cases and decorating them with less expensive design tools or stencils, they could make the case distinctively their own. This was a valuable technique for a manufacturer who could not afford a

After the first sweep of metal compacts were ridiculed and nicknamed "trunks" because they were so large, manufacturers were anxious to advertise their new, thin creations. *Longacre Theatre.*

large financial risk. A variation of this plan was to select a stock compact case and have parts remade in order to give it certain points of distinction. For instance, they could change the compact from a flat to a domed top or vice versa, or reorganize the layout of the interior of the case to give it a new look and a touch of individuality.

Year by year, the cases became smaller, evolving away from the standard round shapes and into more complicated ones. Some became oval, and finally the oblong and square cases and their variations made their way on the market. Smallness became an essential style requisite, and it is logical that manufacturers were eager to advertise their products as "slim" and "sleek."

It was during this stage of the evolution of the compact that manufacturers became aware of design problems. They had discovered that a puff left on the rouge portion of the compact accumulates too much rouge. To rectify the problem, the puff was placed separately in the case at first, but this took up twice the space.

If you've ever wondered why some compacts contain metal mirrors, while others have glass, it is because it was essential to use metal mirrors during manufacturing for compactness. That way, one of the upper areas could be used as a compartment for the rouge, the other for the puff. Later, rouge pots were covered in foil allowing the puff to lie atop without contamination while still saving space. Using a metal mirror also cut back on the weight of the compact.

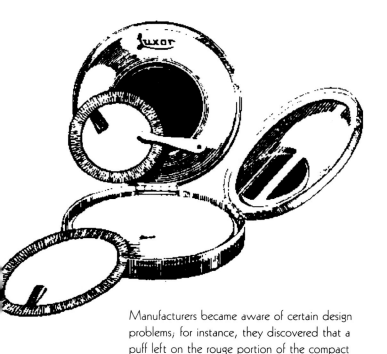

Manufacturers became aware of certain design problems; for instance, they discovered that a puff left on the rouge portion of the compact accumulates too much rouge. To rectify the problem, the puff was placed separately in the case at first. Later, a foil covering was used.

During this time, powder boxes proved to be very popular, but the favorite was still the compact. Rouge was popular in both compact and paste form and lipstick was an essential. Eye shadow and mascara were growing in importance and were packed in individual cases or included in a vanity. More often than not, women would replace an entire compact, rather than send for refills of powder and rouge.

The powder used was to have a tint which blended with the natural color of the skin, giving a bloom to the complexion, and enhancing the beauty of the user. It should have obliterated slight defects, and if perfumed, had to appeal and give added charm. French powders were usually perfumed.

At one time, some of the more common ingredients used in face powder making were starch, talc, and amorphous silica. The silica had good covering powers and absorbed moisture. It also had a fine grade that passed through a silk cloth having as many as 200 meshes per linear inch. Starch was an ingredient that was cause for concern by those who powdered their faces and failed to remove the powder at night. It was suspected that starch, an organic body, may have been entering the pores and fermenting. Rice starch, which has smaller granules, was more widely used and reported to have better results.

Not more than seventy years ago, there were ingredients used in powder making that were discontinued because of health risks or general undesirableness. Among them were: barium sulfate because of the highly toxic character of the barium ion, and orris root, used at one time for making violet powder, but which in certain cases had been believed to promote dermatitis because of a toxic constituent. The color was also a drawback and the powder had a tendency to become damp. Precipitated chalk was an item that was discontinued, although it was inexpensive, because the results were not commendable.

The reverse side depicts a lady, interior reveals puff and metal sifter for loose powder.

Vintage Compacts & Beauty Accessories

A compact press by Stokes that was furnished with engraved or embossed punches to make designs on the compact. The lipstick mold was capable of producing a half gross of lipsticks at one time. *American Perfumer*, 1934.

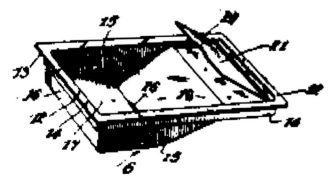

P 1,829,105

The manufacture of face powder was relatively simple in the early thirties, providing efficient machinery was used. Mainly, there were two operations: sifting and mixing. The grinding of the bulk of the materials was unnecessary, if, as commonly was the case, they were bought in the form of sufficiently fine powders. The desired color of the powder was mixed in.

Sifting was effected through silk cloths, as metal cloths would clog. In the case of more expensive products, a double sifting was given. The choice of mesh had to be largely determined by the desired quality of the powder. On average, the sifting cloth would have 120 meshes per linear inch.

Some manufacturers in America later dispensed with sifting, and adopted the plan of passing the already mixed powder through a hammer mill or other type of pulverizer, in which the particles were reduced to a very fine state. The object of sifting, though, was not only to ensure the fineness of the powder, but also to remove impurities.

Various types of sifting machines were used: those in which the cloths were horizontal; and those whose cloth formed the bottom of a tray, which was oscillated to and fro, with the passage of the powder through the sieve facilitated by the presence of a number of rubber balls. In another type, much employed in Great Britain, the powder was brushed or blown through a horizontal, cylindrical sieve, which rotated. Machines were also made to effect both sifting and mixing, and could be fitted with a spraying device for perfuming. Compact presses by Stokes were furnished with engraved or embossed punches to make designs on compact lids. Lipstick molds were capable of producing a half gross of lipsticks at one time.

Once the technicalities of manufacturing the powder was accomplished and the compact was produced, promotion of the product was of utmost concern. Many leading producers experienced considerable success selling cosmetics by launching a series of make-ups with color combinations for their clothes. Capitalizing on fashion in this way encouraged women to buy several cosmetic ensembles instead of only one. Another inducement to encourage a consumer purchase was the souvenir compact.

The "Century of Progress" World's Fair in Chicago in 1933-34 was a surprising place to visit with regard to cosmetics. Amid the freak shows, fakes, ballyhoo, and magic that always makes up a World's Fair, could be found The Oriental Village that reconstructed the life of Egypt, Arabia, and other exotic locations. "The Enchanted Island" consisted of five acres of wonderland including everything from miniature trains to slides; "The Streets of Paris," a slice of the French Capital, with sidewalk cafes, taverns and novelty shops; and "The Home Planning Halls," which showed in detail the "newest" developments in all phases of home building with its developments of prefabricated and composition materials that would permit mass production. Other exhibits featured the world's fastest train from London, the "Royal Scot," and the automobile industry display where cars were turned out from start to finish before the visitor's eyes, with the opportunity to witness the making of tires at the rate of one every ten minutes. The Transportation Building included a historic array of wagons, locomotives, steamships, airplanes, and crude equipment dating back to the 1820s.

Then, there was the Hall of Science which housed most of the exhibits pertaining to cosmetics, drugs, and pharmaceutical products with hundreds of exhibitors including Princess Pat, Ltd. This three story building formed a gigantic letter "U" and had a large circular court. Twelve towering, huge pylons were lighted with concealed gaseous tubes, producing a marvelous lighting effect. From the tower, giant chimes proclaimed the time of day. A selection of wonderful souvenir compacts were sold at the fair.

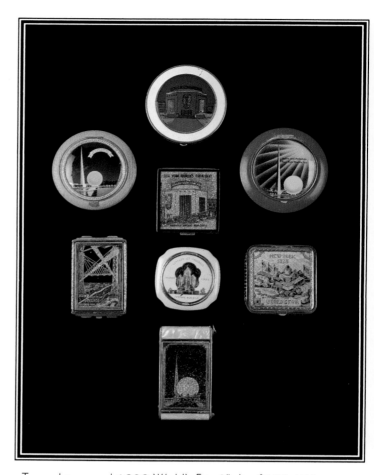

Top: white enamel 1939 World's Fair, 3" dia. $150-175. Second row left: Trylon and Perisphere, 1939, wood with transfer under lid, 3" dia. $125-150. Center: square glitter, 1939, Administration Building by Zell, 2" x 2¼". $100-150. Right: red Bakelite, Trylon and Perisphere written in transfer under lid, 1939, loose powder interior, 3" dia. $175-225. Third row left: Century of Progress, Chicago, 1934 glitter design, camera shaped, 2" x 3". $100-125. Center: white enamel, silver trim, Century of Progress, Chicago, 1934, depicts Federal Building, 2¼" x 2¼". $150-175. Right: New York World's Fair, 1939, tapestry lid, gold mesh pouch, interior reveals Columbia, Fifth Avenue impressed on puff, loose powder, 2½" x 2½". $75-125. Bottom row: camera shaped glitter motif World's Fair, 1939 by Girey, interior reveals a beveled mirror, 2" x 3". $100-125. *From the Collection of Joan Orlen, Photograph by Steven Freeman Photography.*

The Hall of Science at The Century of Progress World's Fair in 1933-34 which housed most of the exhibits pertaining to cosmetics, drugs, and pharmaceutical products. *The American Perfumer.*

New York World's Fair, 1939. Lovely enameled lid depicts various pieces of luggage. Elgin American logo on powder puff and metal case, mirror and loose powder inside. 3" x 2¼". *From the Collection of Joan Orlen, Photograph by Steven Freeman Photography*. $175-250.

One of the exhibits in the Hall was the Franco Beauty Salon whose booth was a popular stop in the opinion of Exposition officials and other exhibitors. Here, women could receive makeovers and were able to purchase a selection of cosmetics, including compacts from large glass front display cases situated in the booth. Skin care booklets and other information were handed out at the booth.

Known as the largest trade fair in the world, the British Industries Fair in 1934 was host to a number of leading cosmetics and perfumery firms located in London and at Castle Bromich, Birmingham. Did you know that the Queen purchased a cosmetic beauty box at this annual event? The box, in nickel plate, was inlaid with plastic and exhibited by Marris's, Ltd.

The Franco Beauty Salon exhibit at the Century of Progress Exposition in Chicago. Here, make-up and souvenir compacts could be purchased. *The American Perfumer*, 1933.

Circa: 1905.

Colorful displays of various cosmetic containers, including rouge pots, cream jars, lipstick containers and compacts molded in Pollopas, Beetle, Bakelite, Crayonne, Bexoid, and other plastic materials, were available at the fair. Of special interest were unusual containers and "new" beauty gadgets, made wholly or partly of these early plastics. The Viscose Development Co., Ltd. showed a type of box molded in one piece, containing two compartments for eyelash mascara and brush respectively, that was fitted with a sliding lid. At the fair, the Impex Co. presented a new patented automatic cream container for the purse that worked on somewhat the same idea as rotating powder sifters.

Marketed by The Altura Pen and Pencil Company, a combination propelling pencil, eyebrow pencil, and lipstick was a newly marketed invention during this Exhibition. Another unusual invention on display was a massage appliance with a reservoir for cream.

The Cosmetics Building at the New York World's Fair in 1939, a huge structure designed to resemble a container for some of the products it displayed inside. World's Fair Expositions offered souvenir compacts.

One of the exhibits at The British Industries Fair in England, the largest trade fair in the world, and host to a number of leading cosmetics and perfumery firms. The Queen purchased a cosmetic beauty box at this event. *The American Perfumer*, 1934.

The first sweep of metal compacts were ridiculed and nicknamed "trunks" because of their large size, while the powder was belittled and called "concrete."

At the New York World's Fair in 1939, a huge structure called The Cosmetics Building was one of the most unusual at the Fair. It was designed to resemble a container for some of the products it displayed inside. An auditorium in the building that was used for the presentation of pageants and cosmetic shows was gained access to by a ramp from the Long Island Railroad Station. Both the 1933-34, and the 1939 World's Fair Expositions offered souvenir compacts.

Some of the souvenir compacts include: lovely enameled compacts depicting various pieces of luggage by Elgin American, those that feature the Trylon and Perisphere, the Adminstration Building by Zell, and the Federal Building. Others had glitter designs and were shaped like cameras, or included Bakelite in the material used to produce the compact.

Then came a tremendous reactionary movement with the entry of "flapjacks" into the market, designed to be on the large side, to sit on the dressing table and be used during the process of applying cosmetics. Women would thrust them into their purses or carry them. However, the flapjack fashion ran its course, and those who got in at the beginning were swept up by the force of its novelty appeal. It came swiftly, skyrocketed, and began to fade out of sight while the cosmetic industry settled back to think up new ways of making compacts plainer and slimmer.

Copying compacts with similar designs as soon as they were deemed successful was also part of the history of compact making. For example, which came first, the Volupté "Petite Boudoir" or the Wadsworth vanity table? How about the many ball shaped compacts or flower basket types?

In 1945, The Elizabeth Arden Powder Room opened its doors to accommodate women in the United States military services. Located at the Service Women's Center in the Hayward Hotel, Los Angeles, California, it was one of several sponsored by the National Fraternity Kappa Kappa Gamma. Here, service women could relax and enjoy the services and products of Elizabeth Arden.

The Elizabeth Arden Powder Room at the Service Women's Center in the Hayward Hotel, Los Angeles, California. Arden made welcome the women in the services of the United States. Circa: 1945.

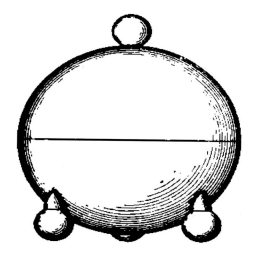

D 94,364

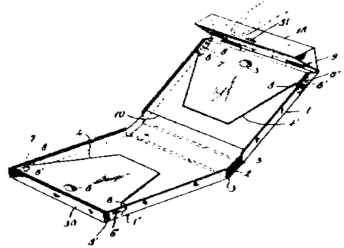

P 1,953,887

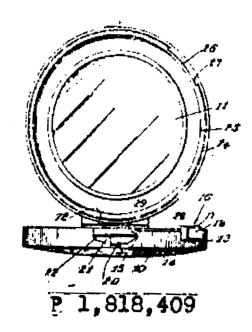

P 1,818,409

Powder Puffs, Patters, & Plis

Even Walt Disney appreciated the popularity of the powder puff and poked humor at its use in his first Oscar winning color cartoon. In the 1932 animation, named *Flowers and Trees*, he illustrates a graceful tree who bends to pluck a fluffy, white dandelion that has turned to seed, and she happily proceeds to powder her face with the weed!

The French produced artistic compacts and puff containers, and also found traces of amusement in them by creating charming figural celluloid powder containers that included puffs attached in untraditional ways. One example is a French celluloid ballerina. The fluffy, feathered puff portion is the bottom of the lady's skirt set to sit on a small celluloid powder bowl atop her legs. In this instance, the bowl is used as a receptacle for loose powder and the fine feather puff resembles a short billowing skirt. The figure, depicted in this unusual way, has hand-painted features with a trace of lipstick and eye make-up. She has a pointed cap and braided hair ending with fluffy balls that match the material around her neck. Her legs are partially covered with pantaloons and the remainder with stockings, and her toes are pointed and posed. The body is made primarily of ivory color except for the bowl, top of her skirt, and the platform she stands on, which are light blue. Her legs are screwed into the bottom of the powder bowl for support. Attention to detail continues when she is turned around and hand-painted accents are detected from behind. Often, a marking impressed into the celluloid can be found stating "Made in France." The French, famous for their ingenious designs, created many of these engaging keepsakes in the Art Deco period, although they are difficult to find today.

Another rare example is a doll with full skirt that has half pockets located around her skirt. This pretty pastel colored doll was made to hold powder puffs in each pocket. Under her skirt, a rigid wire hoop is a necessity so that she could easily stand on a vanity or dressing table. The body of the doll, which consists of only the head to the waist, is made of composition. The doll's face is heavily painted with rouge, lipstick, and eye make-up. She has a pretty curly wig with a pink silk band tied into a bow on one side of her head. This doll did not carry powder, but her puffs, totaling six, continue around the fullness of her skirt, and are round with pretty pastel colored silk tabs attached to each one. The tops of the pockets are reinforced and between each pocket is a delicate pink silk bow. This unusual conversation piece was purchased in gift shops and through mail order catalogs in the 1920s and 1930s.

Judge magazine, 1922.

D 91,818

Detail is shown from behind.

Charming French celluloid ballerina type figure, utilizes the feathery down powder puff as her skirt, and the powder bowl rests atop her legs. Hand painted, two pieces. 8" tall. *Author's Collection*. Very rare.

This lovely pastel colored powder puff doll was made to hold puffs in each pocket of her skirt. The upper portion is made of composition, concealed below is a wire hoop for ease in standing on a vanity or dressing table. Purchased in gift shops and through mail order catalogs in the 1920s and 1930s. 10" tall. *Author's Collection*. Very rare.

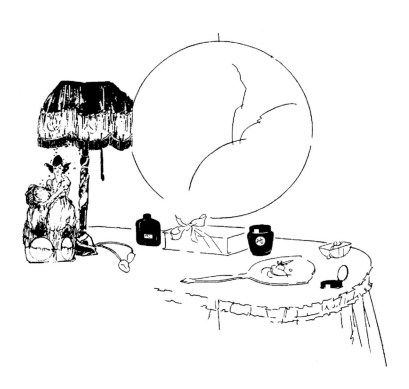

A boxed set of store stock French Plis in various colors, shown opened with puffs exposed. *Lori Landgrebe Antiques.* $125-175 each.

Instructions for the use of the "Houppette Pli."

The rhinestone encrusted French *Houppette Pli*, a celluloid make-up tube containing a feather puff that can be exposed with a twist of the celluloid base. Attached to material encasing the outside of the puff are delicate wires that allow the goose down feathers to expand as they are passed through the pli's channel and exposed. Powder is expelled by unscrewing the other end. "Houppette" is taken from the French word *houppe*, which means *powder puff*. In French, the word *pli* translates to *cover, collapsible*. *The Curiosity Shop.* $145-185.

Plis are French celluloid make-up tubes containing a feather puff that can be exposed with a twist of the celluloid base. Attached to material encasing the outside of the puff are delicate wires that allow the goose down feathers to expand as they are passed through the pli's channel and exposed. Powder is expelled by unscrewing a threaded celluloid cap on the opposite end. The loose powder can be placed in the hand for easy application with the puff.

Plis are found with additional identifying names like "Handi-puff" and "Houppette." "Houppette" is taken from the French word *houppe*, which means *powder puff*. In French, the word *pli* means *to cover, collapsible, yield,* and *to give.* Surprisingly, plis are often found in their original boxes. On a rare occasion, they can also be found with illustrated instructions tucked inside the box. In French, they are described as "*the automatic collapsible, an elegant trinket of small weight that takes up little space, therefore, convenient for the purses of ladies so that they may take care of one's self.*" Plis come in many colors with varying decoration including rhinestones imbedded into the celluloid.

Instructions for the use of the "Houppette Pli."

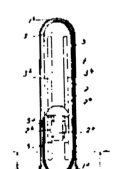

P 1,948,074

Pli in the shape of a doll with hand painted and etched features. Detailed etching is impressed into the celluloid molded clothes, powder is cleverly concealed under the hat. French, circa: 1920s. 4½". *The Curiosity Shop.* $150-225.

Another style of the pli is in the shape of a doll with hand-painted and etched features. Detailed etching is also impressed into the celluloid molded clothes; the powder is cleverly concealed under the hat.

An unusual type of powder puff doll is a German half doll. Composed of china, she has a black molded wig. The headband is painted red, and she, like the other powder puff doll, has painted features showing traces of make-up. The rigid wiring under her skirt is hidden with an additional piece of material. Her dress is simple, and although there are bows between each pocket with reinforcement at the top, the puffs are not original. There are no markings on either of the dolls, and this one was also purchased through the mail or in a gift shop. Both are rare.

A German half doll with powder puff skirt. Made of china, she has a molded wig that is painted black and wears traces of make-up. Purchased through the mail or in a gift shop. 8" tall. Behind her is a silk powder patter. *Author's Collection*. Very rare.

A lovely German half doll made of china perches atop a powder box, her flowing skirt nearly covering the box itself. With typical flapper style attire, she has delicate china legs. The inside of the box, which slides open, contains loose powder and a puff. With great attention to detail, the outside rim of the box is painted gold to match the trim of her skirt and the shine of her heels. 5" tall. Behind her, a peach and blue silk and lace powder patter. *Author's Collection*. Rare.

1630—Madame Pompadour,
quaint and old-fashioned lady,
carries in her gown a powder
compact and puff; she is a
splendid companion and looks
her best on the dressing table.
Hand decorated and packed
with appropriate card. This
little lady comes 3½ inches
high...................... .50

Pohlson Gifts.

5336—A Beautiful Vanity Lady.
Adorable for dressing table. Made
of lovely frosted glass. She is just
6 inches tall, and beneath her flowing skirts is puff and ample space
for powder. Safely packed.. 2.00

Pohlson Gifts.

A French novelty powder bowl made entirely of celluloid depicts a man and woman in a romantic pose. He is quite debonair, with a molded celluloid black tuxedo and gold painted collar and cuffs, a black mustache and dark painted hair. She has a simple hand-painted pink dress that meets just above the knee. The female figure stands atop a fluffy goose feather puff inside the box, although an appropriately placed slit in the celluloid lid makes it appear as though she stands on the lid. When the container is opened, the man, who stands atop the powder bowl lid is moved away from the woman with his arms open. When the lid is closed and fastened with a small moveable celluloid closure, the man stands quite near the woman, his arms outstretched for an embrace. The expression on her face and the placement of her arms seems to depict an element of surprise. All of the clever fittings used to make this piece are of molded celluloid.

A lovely German half doll powder is a unique collectible and hard to find. Made of china, she perches atop a powder box, her flowing skirt nearly covering the piece itself. Her typical flapper style attire consists of a striped hat and a polka-dot shirt with a pink scarf also molded from china. Delicate china legs are crossed and jut out from the box. Her shoes are painted gold. The detailed skirt is constructed of peach colored material with an elaborate gold, peach, and black striped ruffled trim. Material under her skirt continues over the entire top of the powder container like a pin cushion, and delicate legs are sewn into the top of it, yet are concealed under the outer skirt. The inside of the container, which slides open, holds loose powder and a puff. With great attention to detail, the outside rim is painted gold to match the trim of her skirt and the shine of her heels.

A French novelty powder bowl made entirely of celluloid depicts a debonair man and a young woman in a romantic pose. The female figure stands atop a fluffy goose feather powder puff inside the box, although an appropriately placed slit makes it appear as though she stands on the lid. Shown closed, the man stands quite near the woman, his arms outstretched for an embrace. All of the clever fittings used to make this piece are of molded celluloid. 7" tall. *Author's Collection*. Very rare.

When the box is opened, the man, who stands atop the powder bowl lid, moves away from the woman with his arms open.

The French designed colorful powder containers that resemble miniature hat boxes. Dark blues, pinks, yellows, and a variety of other colors form the deep bottoms and short lids of these powder receptacles. Inside, the down puffs with silk tops are attached to composition doll heads with painted flapper hats and heavily painted faces. Other character heads, including harlequins, have been found attached to puffs in this manner. In other instances, the puffs can be found with simple non-figural white china, metal, or celluloid tops. It is not unusual to find a character or doll topped puff either without a box or with a box whose color has faded through the years.

French designed powder boxes. One resembles a miniature hat box. Inside is a down puff with a silk top attached to a composition doll head with a flapper hat. Also shown is a down feather powder puff with a simple celluloid top and a deep celluloid powder container. *Author's Collection*. Left, rare; right, $50-75.

Powder patters with flower basket embellishments, trimmed in silk and black lace. 4" dia. *Author's Collection*. $125-150.

5688—A Powder Patter, made of two-toned ribbon in the form of a rose, hand made and finished with cream silk lace. A lovely gift any woman will appreciate **1.00**

4412—A Patience Powder Patter. Welcome aid to daintiness. Patience, tall and fair, with a touch of her fluffy puff, will dust your favorite powder over your shoulders **1.00**

Powder patters advertised in their original boxes, hand made with silk and lace. Circa: 1920s. *Pohlson gift catalog.*

Powder patters in two very different designs. The purple has a mushroom style ribbing done in silk with a velvet bow, the other a silk checkerboard crosshatching motif. 4" dia. *Author's Collection.* $125-150.

Powder patters were available in a variety of designs including doll-like characters faces. Shown with a small vanity mirror in a similar motif. 4" dia. *Author's Collection.* Left, $20-40; right, $125-150.

Sometimes referred to as "puffs on sticks," these delicate little luxuries of the past were originally called *powder patters* and were often found in delightful gift catalogs containing a wide range of interesting novelties like figural pin cushions, tape measures, ladies' handkerchiefs, and flower basket shaped shade pulls. In the twenties and thirties, patters, often round or oval shaped and handmade of ribbon and lace in various shades of silk, contained bulbous puffs. The patter portion sometimes emulated roses, flowers, and infrequently, fruit.

On occasion, a patter would come with a matching mirror. In this instance, silk, ribbon, lace, or various other materials would be combined to create a similar or matching theme, but one of the stick's tops would turn over to reveal a mirror instead of a powder patter. They were advertised as "a welcome aid to daintiness, a gift any woman will appreciate." During a time when a hand sewn leather bill fold would cost six dollars, you could expect to pay only one to two dollars for a powder patter in its box with a gift card.

A collection of various silk and lace powder patters decorated with various bows and silk flowers, used for loose powder. Stems are wrapped in silk ribbon. *Author's Collection*. $120-180.

An appreciation for the humor in powdering one's nose. *Judge* magazine, 1921.

The Patience Powder Patter came boxed with a charming card that read: "Patience, tall and fair, with a touch of her fluffy puff, will dust your favorite powder over your shoulders." Manufacturers who had a keen eye for fashion took advantage of the opportunity to create a patter necessary for the low-cut and backless dress styles of the day. 3" x 6". *The Curiosity Shop.* $125-175.

Bejeweled and gilt lady sits atop a blue glass powder bowl. 4½" x 6". *Author's Collection.* $150-200.

The *Patience Powder Patter* came boxed with a card that read: "Patience, tall and fair, with a touch of her fluffy puff, will dust your favorite powder over your shoulders." Manufacturers who had a keen eye for fashion, took advantage of the opportunity to create a patter necessary for the low-cut and backless dress styles of the day. Mistaken for shoe buffs, the type of patter that was used to apply powder to the lady's back sometimes had a different shape than that used on her face. While fluffy and soft, like the types used to powder faces, they may resemble a number eight or shoe shape rather than a simple oval or round form.

It is fun to try to find patters with fetching sayings on small slips of paper that they were once sold with. As with most antiques or collectibles, those found unused and in the original box are even more sought after. Due to their delicate composition and difficulty to find, powder patters found in good condition today are worth considerably more than their original cost.

A silk patter and matching beveled glass mirror in a peach motif. Fruit themes in patters are difficult to find, as are matching sets with mirrors and patters found on the reverse. 5½" x 2½" dia. *Author's Collection*. Rare.

Vintage Compacts & Beauty Accessories

Fulton Theatre.

POWDER PUFFS that are BETTER MADE

Unique wallets for perfume vials and vanities also our specialty.

Our prices and quality must be right.

Our capacity is 100,000 units per day.

FURLAGER MANUFACTURING CO., INC.
116 WEST 14th STREET, NEW YORK, N. Y.
"Service Via The Golden Rule"

Some companies made their livelihoods by producing and distributing powder puffs which were sold to compact manufacturers to be included in the compact receptacle. *The American Perfumer*, 1931.

Three pink silk and lace powder patters including an oval one. From 3½" to 4". *The Curiosity Shop.* $125-150.

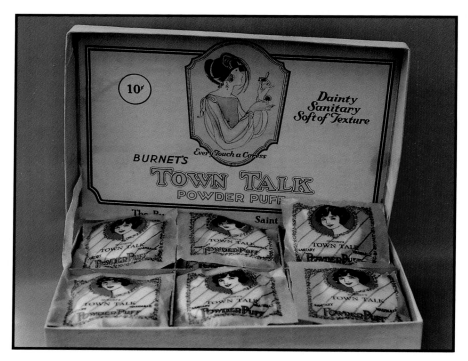

"Town Talk" powder puffs in pre-packaged, store stock box, originally selling for ten cents each. *Author's Collection.* $150-200 set.

Dressing table powder boxes, bowls, and jars were popular gifts in a wide range of designs. From four inch transparent celluloid powder boxes with velour puffs, detailed with rose decorations, glass powder bowls, and moire silk folding compacts with mirrors to six inch frosted glass vanity ladies who conceal puffs with ample space for powder beneath flowing skirts, dressing table adornments were popular keepsakes. Decorated gift cards enclosed with some powder items would read, "A bit of loveliness my lady will deem this."

The decade dubbed "the romantic thirties" according to the costumers claimed romance was sending women to beauty parlors to acquire a blush that was softer and more natural than the hard, clear color produced by rouge. Specialists devised stimulants for the face that were like exterior cocktails, whipping the blood to the surface and leaving the skin glowing and clear.

Dorothy Gray invented a unique instrument that was specially made to apply stimulation to the facial muscles without irritating the skin. Patented in 1923, it is an odd looking contraption that has a handle attached to a metal band and round patter.

Elizabeth Arden designed a comparable looking instrument with a similar theory in the early thirties. Given regular care and exercise of the facial skin by patting it, the blood would come dancing to the cheeks, invigorating the tissues and clearing the skin. Through her staff, she offered individual consultations and her Venetian toilet preparations were sold at a variety of exclusive shops.

The Arden Venetian Patter was an unconventional device used for home treatment when following the Arden Muscle-Strapping, Skin-Toning Method. The round, flat patter, with a unique flexible handle, was reported to give accurate patting strokes with the same resiliency of a skilled Arden Salon's expert's fingers. The patter was meant to be used together with other Arden products such as skin tonic or astringent. The user was to wrap a moistened pad of absorbent cotton over the round patter, fasten it with a rubber band, dip it in the tonic and pat with upward movements. It sold for five dollars.

Although Arden did not sanction the use of massage, she endorsed what she termed "the molding of facial muscles by clever, scientific manipulation." The procedure consisted of a smart and rapid patting following the line of muscles of the face and neck. The patting was in an upward motion, presumably to lift the muscles and help overcome their natural tendency to droop and sag. If accomplished correctly, it would, she indicated, stimulate circulation and increase the functional activities of the tissues. Arden had locations in large cities all over the United States and shops in London, Berlin, Paris, Madrid, and Rome.

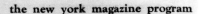

4634—Every one uses powder. Therefore, this **Powder Jar,** which, indeed, is exquisite in every detail. Beautiful in shape. Fashioned of white frosted glass with decoration in wild roses. Inside is a pink velour puff trimmed with hand-made silk roses. Jar is 3¼ inches in diameter. Guaranteed to reach you in perfect condition. 1.50

Pohlson Gifts.

Make-up ensemble; rouge, lip rouge, eye shadow, eyebrow pencil and mascara in rich chest. Opens into modernistic tabouret. Sparkling in hammered gold, black and red effect. Smartest gift imaginable. $3.

The GESTURE OF BEAUTY

THESE SOPHISTICATES . . . alluring, lovely women who intrigue the senses with flawless beauty . . . what is their secret? First the corrective creams which accomplish true skin perfection . . . then selection of only the most perfect make-up. They make the gesture of beauty grandly . . . as a consummate art.

Powder! There are dozens, scores, hundreds. But there is only one powder in the world made with a

25

Princess Pat make-up ensemble in hammered gold, black, and red chest. It sold for three dollars. For You—Exquisite Beauty, *1932.*

ℰLIZABETH ARDEN understands the exquisite care of the skin and knows that faces require regular care and exercise in order that the blood may come dancing to the cheeks to invigorate the tissues and clear the skin. She understands bodies, too, and has created a series of exercises to keep you wide awake—and slim—and lovely!

A Personal Consultation will be gladly arranged for you, without any obligation. Please telephone Plaza 5847.

Elizabeth Arden's Venetian Toilet Preparations are on sale at the smart shops everywhere

ELIZABETH ARDEN

673 FIFTH AVENUE, NEW YORK

Boston	Philadelphia	Chicago	Detroit
San Francisco	Los Angeles	Atlantic City	Washington

LONDON BERLIN PARIS MADRID ROME

Elizabeth Arden designed an instrument in the early thirties called the Venetian Patter, with the theory that with regular care and exercise of the facial skin by patting it, blood would come dancing to the cheeks, invigorating the tissues and clearing the skin. *The New Magazine Program.*

An indispensable combination for toning and building relaxed tissue

The Elizabeth Arden Venetian Patter shown with other products in that line. Although Arden did not sanction the use of massage, she endorsed what she termed as "the molding of facial muscles by clever scientific manipulation." *The Quest of the Beautiful,* circa 1931.

The Princess Pat "Vaniteen" is a metal container that carries a combination of rouge and automatic loose powder dispenser. To release the powder, the Vaniteen point is pressed onto the puff. It sold retail for one dollar and was advertised as spill-proof. Handsomely finished in gold and richly embossed, it measures only three inches long. Store owners were offered a silver colored display tree for the holidays that could display a dozen Vaniteens. Or, if the store owner preferred, the company would gift box each in holly and snowflake boxes with satin lining.

Princess Pat powder compact with rouge. Puff is impressed with logo. 1½" dia. *The Curiosity Shop*. $35-50.

Princess Pat Rouge changes slightly on the skin to harmonize with underlying flesh tones. Thus each shade is natural.

Princess Pat rouge. 1932.

The decade dubbed "the romantic thirties," according to the costumiers, claimed romance was persuading women to acquire a softer and more natural blush than the hard, clear color produced by rouge. Specialists devised stimulants for the face that were like exterior cocktails, whipping the blood to the surface and leaving the skin glowing and clear.

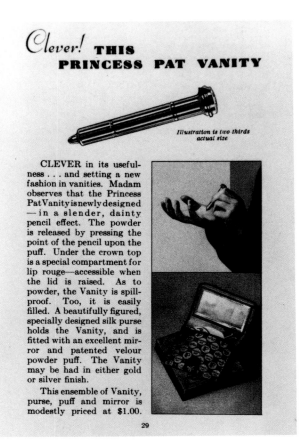

Clever! THIS PRINCESS PAT VANITY

Illustration is two-thirds actual size

CLEVER in its usefulness . . . and setting a new fashion in vanities. Madam observes that the Princess Pat Vanity is newly designed — in a slender, dainty pencil effect. The powder is released by pressing the point of the pencil upon the puff. Under the crown top is a special compartment for lip rouge—accessible when the lid is raised. As to powder, the Vanity is spillproof. Too, it is easily filled. A beautifully figured, specially designed silk purse holds the Vanity, and is fitted with an excellent mirror and patented velour powder puff. The Vanity may be had in either gold or silver finish.

This ensemble of Vanity, purse, puff and mirror is modestly priced at $1.00.

29

For You—Exquisite Beauty, 1932.

A PUFF FOR EVERY PURPOSE

Valmont

Patented

FOR your dusting powder, there is nothing better than our PURSE PUFF as illustrated. It has added color and attractiveness and an effective hand hold which makes it comfortable to use.

The newer compacts call for odd shaped puffs and a color imprint to identify your package. We are equipped to make all shapes of puffs and imprint them at very moderate costs. Our Printing Department has a capacity of 500 gross per day, which means service without delay.

OXZYN COMPANY
VALMONT DIVISION
154 11th Ave.   New York City

The American Perfumer, 1932.

The Powder Puff is the title of a little known advice booklet printed in 1933 offering make-up and powder hints. Advertised as "a monthly good looks letter from the Health and Beauty department of *Good Housekeeping*," and available to the public, this no-nonsense, typed periodical contained recommendations for every skin type and corresponding make-up choices. Written by Ruth Murrin, the *Good Housekeeping* Beauty Editor, references to name brand powders and cosmetics are made including: Dorothy Gray, Coty, Tangee, Ponds, Max Factor, Kathleen Mary Quinlan, Yardley, Princess Pat, Houbigant, Harriet Hubbard Ayer, Elizabeth Arden, Woodbury, Guerlain, Armands and La Blache. The booklet reminds consumers to look for the Bureau of Foods, Sanitation and Health's oval seal when buying cosmetics and toilet preparations.

The Powder Puff, an advice booklet offering make-up and powder hints. Written by Ruth Murrin, editor of the Health and Beauty department of *Good Housekeeping*, printed in 1933.

A boxed store stock silk powder puff, still encased in cellophane. 3½" dia. *The Curiosity Shop*. $25-45.

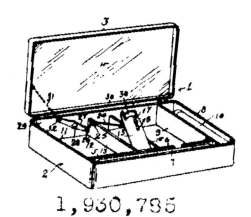

1,930,735

The American Perfumer, 1932.

Theodore W. Foster & Brothers manufactured a lovely sterling and enameled lipstick and powder pencil which measured between four and six inches. The powder section has a hinged opening on the opposite side of the lip rouge. They are Old English finished and sold wholesale between four fifty and ten dollars. Enameled lip rouges and perfume receptacles could also be purchased separately.

A company called Burnet's in St. Louis, Missouri, distributed sanitary, washable "Town Talk" powder puffs in pink and white. Each was wrapped in cellophane and displayed in the store in an illustrated box. They sold for ten cents each.

It is hard to imagine that some companies made the majority of their livelihoods by producing and distributing powder puffs which were sold to compact manufacturers to be included in the compact receptacle. One example is the Oxzyn Company in New York and Canada that produced sterilized compact puffs made of lambskin, wool, and velour. A large part of their business was manufacturing puffs, but they also produced their own line of rouges, powders, eye shadows, eye brow pencils, and other waterproof cosmetics.

Powder puff making was serious business in the early part of the twentieth century and the Powder Puff Manufacturer's Association, Inc. was the first organization of these manufacturers in the United States. Committees were appointed to draft conditions of wages, hours, and sanitary standards under the Wagner Industrial Recovery Bill. Some leading members in the industry in June of 1933 were: Jeanette Powder Puffs, Inc., Oxzyn Co., Downy-Puff Corp., and The Hygienol Co., Inc.

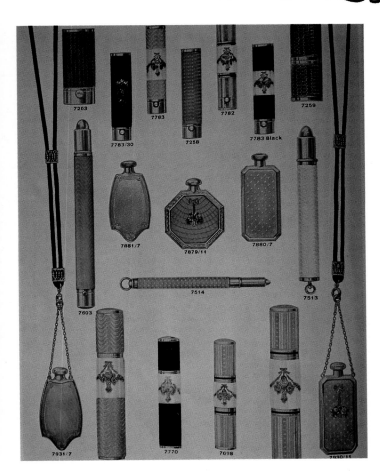

Theodore W. Foster & Brother's sterling and enameled lipstick and powder pencil measuring between 4"-6". The powder section has a hinged opening on the opposite side of the lip rouge. Old English finished, selling wholesale between four fifty and ten dollars. Enameled lip rouges and perfume receptacles could be purchased separately. *The Foster Blue Book*, 1925-26.

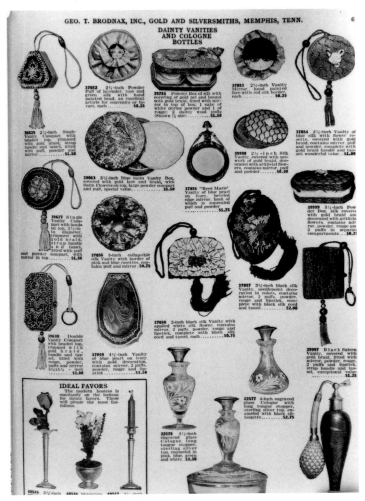

George T. Brodnax, Inc., 1926.

The "Norida" and an unsigned compact with metal sifter. 2¼" dia. Shown with cosmetic mirrors. *Author's Collection*. Top, $50-65; bottom, $65-75; mirrors, $75-150.

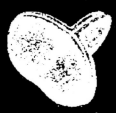

D 85,828

#85,828 Patent for powder puff to The A.J. Donahue Corporation, Milford, Connecticut. Filed October 14, 1931.

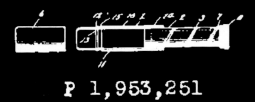

P 1,953,251

Chapter Three

Figurals & Novelties

The fabulous figural and novelty compacts that are so sought out today evolved gradually as manufacturers kept a keen eye out for fashion trends. Eccentric items like the furry Schuco monkey compact with the concealed lipstick in its neck, or the elegant Volupté "Golden Gesture" hand shaped compact, invented by Ruth Warner Mason, were not the first novelty compacts to be introduced to the market. Instead, retail inclinations were carefully considered and cautiously tested before these whimsical fancies were designed, manufactured, and marketed.

Shown open to reveal a hidden lipstick in its neck, powder, puff, and mirror in the belly is the Schuco miniature monkey compact. $400-600.

Fur-like material covers its body, the paws are felt. Circa: 1920. 3¾". *The Curiosity Shop.*

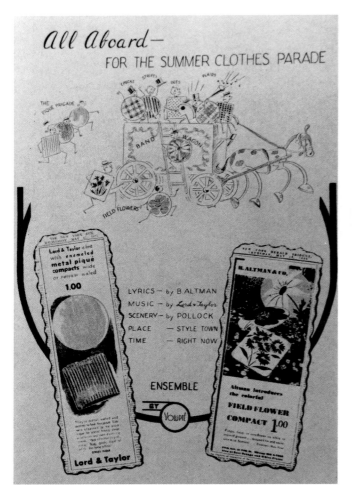

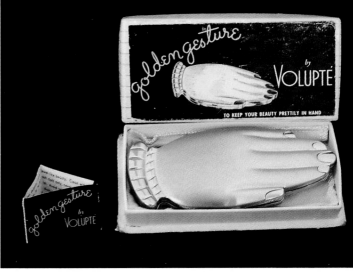

Volupté "Golden Gesture" hand shaped compact with felt cover in presentation box. "To keep your beauty prettily in hand." 4½" x 2". *The Curiosity Shop.* $175-225.

Compacts were tailored to match outfits. Advertisements like this were clever merchandising stunts designed to promote assembling accessories not only for the convenience of the customer, but also to inspire additional purchases. Whether the choice was for checks, polka dots, plaids, stripes, or pastels, the novelty compact department of the five and dime store could fill the demand. *The American Perfumer*, 1933.

Some of the novelty vanities of 1933 with textured and fabric lids. At the top left is the Volupté "Peacock," a handmade square compact with 794 individual mirrors covering it that was flown to the Countess of Jersey at Osterley Park, Isleworth, England. *The American Perfumer.*

In the summer of 1933, compacts were tailored to match outfits. A clever merchandising stunt was to assemble accessories not only for the convenience of the customer but also to inspire additional purchases. Who could resist a "compact to match" when thus tantalizingly presented? Whether the choice was for checks, polka dots, plaids, stripes, or pastels, the novelty compact department could fill the demand.

Clothing and compact matching went even further. Not only were fabric colors and patterns duplicated in vanities, but also the fabrics themselves were. The finely ribbed surface of piqué was easily carried out in metal, so that a woman could not only match her blue piqué sports frock with a blue vanity—but with a blue piqué vanity! One manufacturer made actual inlays of linen on the covers of their compacts; the more usual thing however, and the more practical, was to lightly emboss the surface of the metal to create a linen-like effect.

Summer country flower designs on compacts became popular because the latest whimsy during the early part of the thirties was a luxurious gown with a pretty flower cluster which bobbed around under the chin. Continuing the flower motif, but varying it to suit, the painted hothouse flower instead of the country grown one also enhanced the lid of the vanity. The stately lily, for instance, enjoyed a vogue as decoration on boudoir dressing sets and offered another suggestion for compact design.

Fetching nautical designs on vanity cases were inspired by the popularity of the yachting type of costume. The simplicity and universal appeal of sail boats, anchors, and all the other sea related paraphernalia made upbeat and successful motifs for decorations. Similar to the popular country flower pattern, some of these nautical designs were so clever that stores bid for the exclusive rights on certain favorites. Later, in the 1940s, these nautical designs as well as patriotic motif compacts filled novelty stores. Hat shaped compacts consisted of the early plastic U.S. khaki and brown colored Army officer's cap with a gold foil brim crest, the popular early plastic blue and white U.S. Navy officer's cap with embossed crest, and the bronzed metal Air Force officer's cap with a faux jeweled Armed Forces eagle on the lid, which were available at the five and dime store. Also manufactured were compacts with faux jeweled "V's" for victory; American flag motif compacts; those adorned with eagles, the Statue of Liberty, and "U.S. Zone" maps; and other red, white, and blue embellished compacts. These were made by a variety of manufacturers including Zell, Volupté, Elgin American, and Henriette, to name a few.

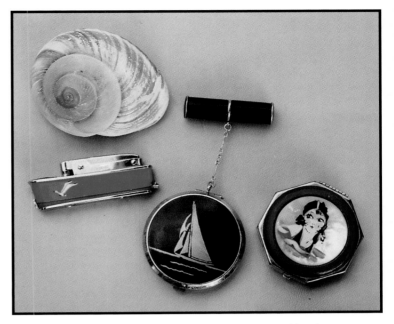

Fetching nautical designs on vanity cases were inspired by the popularity of the yachting motif clothing. The simplicity and universal appeal of sail boats, anchors, and all the other sea related paraphernalia made upbeat and successful motifs for decorations. Left: black enameled sailboat decorated powder/rouge compact with attached lipstick. 2" dia. Hand painted bathing beauty with metal sifter inside. 2¼" dia. *The Curiosity Shop*. Left, $100-125; right, $125-150.

Large loose powder compact designed to resemble an officer's cap in presentation box to be used on a vanity table. 7" dia. Also: red, white, & blue plastic Navy officer's cap with gold foil crest. 3" dia. Circa: 1940s. *From the Collection of Kay Miguez, Photograph by Miguez Photography*. Left, $125-175; right, $65-75.

Women also began turning to wood in their accessories. Hats, belts, and purses went wooden—and, of course, so did compacts. In this instance, the wooden vanity did the pioneering and set the pace for other wooden accessories. Wooden beads, bracelets, clips, and pins, some of which could be hand-crafted at home, had now joined the all-wood ensemble so that a woman could work out an entire costume scheme in her favorite grain. Zebra wood, Oriental walnut, red cedar, hardwood, and bird's eye maple, furnished some beautiful finishes for these attractive novelties. Strands of perfectly huge gray pearls that topped the winter costume were coupled with gray wood vanities—and the effect on shoppers was amazing!

A clever duo in 1933 was the combination of wood with metal, often in cloisonné finish. The cloisonné was usually used as an all-over decorative cover for the powder and rouge compartments although brightly enameled metal panels on either side of a square shaped compact case of wood added a new dimension. The apparent purpose of this combination of materials was to relieve the "woodenness" of the plain, unadorned compact. A similar outcome was achieved by unusual grain effects when the center of the case was cut in one way and the border in another. In addition to real wood, simulated wood effects were also produced on metal. Leather graining, snakeskin, and sharkskin were similarly reproduced on metal. These compacts were not such a high risk for manufacturers since they were not as seasonal as fabric covered compacts.

Copper compacts were an interesting departure from the garden variety of the enamel case. Striking and smart, they blended beautifully with women's copper purses, novelty jewelry, and copper colored dresses, proving to be popular in the fall. Much later, Avon distributed the coppertone "Lucky Penny" lip gloss compact that was in the shape of, and patterned after, the rare 1909S V.D.B. Lincoln cent. Originally, the penny was issued to honor the 100th anniversary of Lincoln's birth and was designed by Victor D. Brenner. Although the compact resembles copper, it is made of a very lightweight plastic with a screw-off top. Inside, there are two compartments for companion shades of lip gloss meant to be applied with a fingertip.

If you are wondering how compact manufacturers were able to obtain advance fashion information on costume colors and fabrics so that a new crop of vanities could appear on the market simultaneously with the newest clothes, the answer is it was not that difficult. Fall and winter favored certain shades of grays, greens, browns, reds, and black that could be reproduced on metal and in fabric, while summer vanities were brighter in color. Roman stripes, candy stripes, and other striped variations were appearing on velvets and satins, and lent themselves easily to copying by the compact manufacturer, who kept in tune with the latest fashions along with an awareness of the season in which they were striving to market in.

The "Lucky Penny" lip gloss compact by Avon, patterned after the rare 1909S V.D.B. Lincoln cent. The penny was issued to honor the 100th anniversary of Lincoln's birth, designed by Victor D. Brenner. Screw-off top. Inside, two compartments for companion shades of lip gloss to be applied with a fingertip. Copper colored plastic, 2" dia. Also shown: heavy metal perfume container. 1" dia. *The Curiosity Shop.* Left, $100-150; right, $50-60.

Silver and silver-like metals were the longtime favorites for vanity cases until gold staged a return to favor, ousting the previous preference. One collection of compacts shown in gold takes its inspiration from the old fashioned, ornate gold bracelet. Another group is promoted with the phrase, "Brighten up your costume with a gold compact," and depicts gold colored compacts with a ribbed surface to emulate the texture of fabric. Woolens discreetly patterned with gold sequins, thread laces embroidered in gold, and bright gold patterned fabrics resembling supple brocades, easily tied in with refreshing gold novelty compacts.

F.J. Company goldtone compact/bracelet combination. Black enameled central disc with raised flowers on cuff's shoulders. 1⅞" dia. *The Curiosity Shop.* $250-325.

Evening vanities boasted seed pearl decorations, the covers of which were composed of circle after circle of tiny, faux pearls, with the bottoms enameled white, and the sides of gold. Lamé vanities were also designed for evening use. Placing glass on the outside as well as inside of the compact was another novel idea. Tiny pieces of mirror casting myriad reflections in an enchanting manner on top of the vanity case flashed everywhere. A simple idea that made these startling vanities add a smart note to any evening ensemble also made it unnecessary to have a matching case for every outfit.

In 1934, Volupté created a compact called the "Peacock," a handmade square compact with 794 individual mirrors covering it. It was flown to the Countess of Jersey at Osterley Park, Isleworth, England, who was prominent in British social circles. The delivery by a Transatlantic Freight Plane was an opportunity for Volupté to improve its service, and to catch the eye of the alert public. The promotional delivery was engineered by Jack Pollock, Sales Manager of Volupté, Inc., New York.

Leaving little ground uncovered, the art world was also investigated for new ideas in compact design with both charming and ludicrous results. Reproductions of famous paintings, such as those of Watteau, often decorated the cover of a vanity. As an all-over lid covering or occasionally executed in a medieval looking medallion, when skillfully administered, these reproductions lent a quaintness that appealed to the consumer. The humorist Soglow struck a clever art note entirely different from serious reproductions. Capricious and clever, the amusing "Peeping Tom" compacts awakened an inspiration in the quest for new and unusual compact ideas.

Compacts were not only made to match outfits, but they were also created to accessorize when taking on the appearance of jewelry. Designers in Paris created an unusual round clip resembling an oversized button, that for all apparent purposes simply adorned the ladies' gown—until she disengaged it and began to powder her nose! Made for those who travel lightly, this miniature compact with a tiny mirror has all the fittings. It contains powder, mirror, and puff. Although not greatly received at the time since it was contrived as an expression of a new whim or fancy, it is rare and appreciated more today.

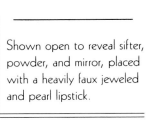

Shown open to reveal sifter, powder, and mirror, placed with a heavily faux jeweled and pearl lipstick.

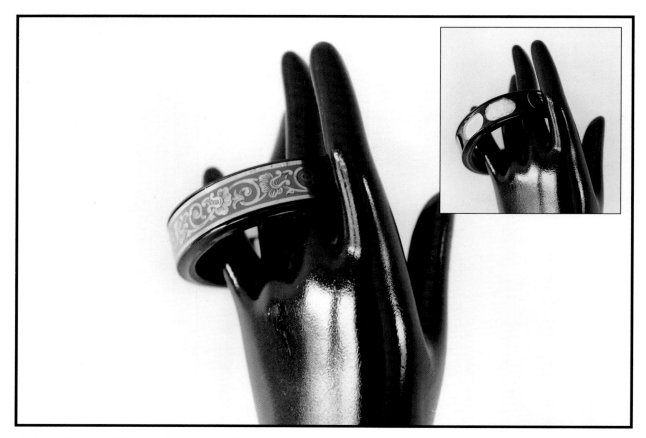

Marlowe Company "Parisienne" early plastic/Bakelite compact/bracelet combination in dark green. The metal band slides to gain access to interior cosmetics. It originally sold for $2.20. ¾" dia. Also shown open to reveal two mirrors and five cosmetic containers including rouge, powder, lipstick, and three puffs. *The Curiosity Shop.* $225-325.

Other examples of jewelry/compact combinations are compact bracelets, ranging from early plastic and Bakelite bangles, to metal cuffs heavily adorned with faux jewels and enameled flowers, which were popular conversation pieces of their day. Some of the metal bracelets are gilt with large round enameled discs and fancy raised floral designs on either side, while others are gold metal with a rectangular shaped compact opening that conceals a puff with powder and a mirror, one boasting a dual opening with a curved comb and lip smudge.

French designers produced the "Parisienne" Bakelite compact distributed by the Marlowe Company. It consists of a combination metal band that slides aside to reveal five oval cosmetic compartments including powder, rouge, lip smudge and three puffs. The color of the plastic varies from cherry red, lime, hunter green, burgundy, and butterscotch, to name a few. The metal bands were available in at least two decorative styles. These compacts are easily recognizable since the manufacturer molded the name inside the bracelet. They were advertised in gift catalogs and sold for approximately two dollars in the early Forties. A portion of the advertisement read: "A turn of the gold decorated band transforms this unique bracelet into a complete make-up kit."

Marlowe Company "Parisienne" in red. Plastic colors varied to include lime and dark green, burgundy, and butterscotch, to name just a few. Metal bands were available in at least two decorative styles. ¾" dia. *The Curiosity Shop.* $250-350.

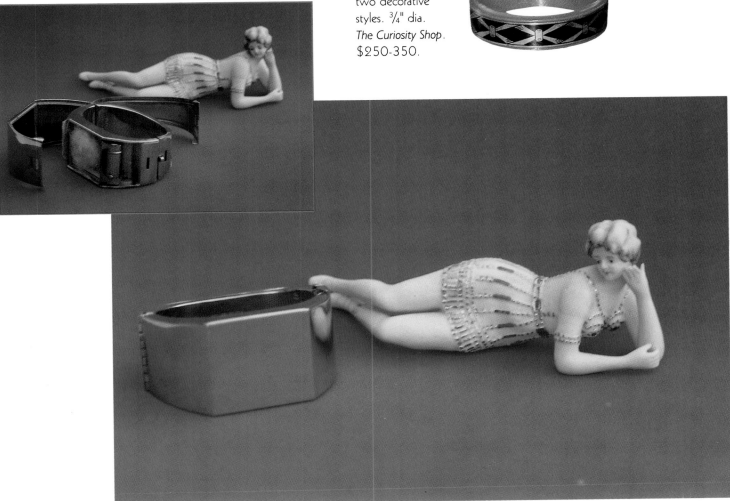

Zama French cuff goldtone bracelet compact with dual hinged openings. 1½" x 2¾" dia. Interior is fitted with curved comb, mirror, powder, rouge, lipstick tube, and eye smudge. Rare. *Lori Landgrebe Antiques.*

Goldtone hinged bracelet/compact combination with faux jewels and enameled flowers. Shown open, it reveals mirror and puff. 2" x 1½". *The Curiosity Shop*. $250-350.

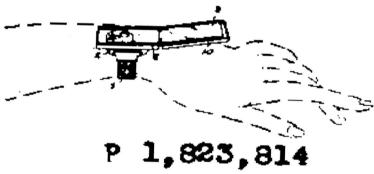

P 1,823,814

Patent for bracelet compact placed by Anthony F. Aiello, Brooklyn, New York, Filed March 14, 1930.

Evans lady golfer cuff/compact combination. Silvered metal with a hand painted female golfer under a round glass lid. Inside can be found powder, puff, and mirror. This bracelet has double appeal, for both the compact/bracelet enthusiast, and the golf devotee. 2" wide. *The Curiosity Shop*. Very rare.

Another rare silvered metal compact bracelet, made by the Evans Manufacturing Company, has a hand painted female golfer under a round glass lid. The cuff style band has openwork on both sides. Inside could be found powder, puff and mirror. This bracelet has double appeal for both the compact/bracelet enthusiast and the golf devotee.

Oval and round top ring compacts sold in novelty catalogs for one dollar. They were made of hinged metal and included powder, puff, and a tiny sized mirror. Pendant necklaces also concealed powder and puff. Disguised with cameo fronts, colorful enameled decoration, or black enameled figural silhouettes, many came with linked neckchains. Easy to lift and open, one could take a quick and discreet check of make-up with these handy pieces.

Ladies' compact canes or sticks came in an assortment of designs. The metal variety have hinged lids that lift open to reveal mirror, powder, and puff. Ivory, early plastic, and ceramic styles were usually threaded and screwed open. Sterling and metal lids can be adorned with Oriental or Siamese scenes. Shafts can be found in a variety of materials including bamboo, ebony, and mahogany. With plain or fancy collars, metal ferrule protectors cover the ends of the sticks. Equally rare is the compact/parasol combination that contains a compact in the handle.

Enameled Opera Locket Compacts

Very ornamental as a style accessory, made even thinner than the old style lockets, yet concealed within is a large cake of powder, a puff and a full size non-breakable mirror. The workmanship and finish are faultless, every detail has been handled in a most careful manner, making the finished article really a work of art. In fancy gift boxes. The illustrations show actual size.

GIFTS THAT LAST

GIFTS THAT LAST

CLOISONNE ENAMELED OPERA COMPACT
Genuine cloisonne enameled "Dancing Girl," in soft pastel shades. White gold filled locket and 24 inch fancy link chain. Contains full size powder cake, puff and non-breakable mirror. The back of locket is covered with a brocade design.
No. 8647 Each................$9.40

HARD ENAMELED OPERA COMPACT
Black enameled "Colonial Belle" and border, on silver background. Yellow gold filled locket and 24 inch chain. Contains full size cake powder, puff and non-breakable mirror. Back of locket is covered with a brocade design.
No. 8648 Each................$5.00

CLOISONNE ENAMELED OPERA COMPACT
Beautiful cloisonne enameled "Colonial Girl," in dainty pastel colors. Yellow gold filled locket and 24 inch chain. Contains full size cake powder, powder puff and non-breakable mirror. The back of locket is covered with a brocade design.
No. 8646 Each................$7.00

HARD ENAMELED OPERA COMPACT
Black enameled "Beau & Belle" on silver enameled background. Yellow gold filled locket and 24 inch chain. Contains full size cake powder, puff and non-breakable mirror. Back of locket is covered with a brocade design.
No. 8649 Each................$5.00

THE VANI-MIST TRIPLE VANITY

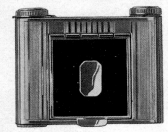

Showing Vani-Mist Open

The Vani-Mist is a new and interesting toilet accessory. It combines all necessities into one. In it may be carried loose powder, rouge, lipstick and perfume. Made of solid nickel silver, straight line engine turned. Front is of black French enamel. A turn of right hand knurled knob towards you reveals the lipstick—which when used as a plunger on the spring underneath, operates perfume spray when left hand knurled knob is opened. Small illustration shows interior arrangement. Full instructions accompany each Vani-Mist. In fancy gift box. Size 2½x1¾ inches.
No. 8652 Each...$10.50

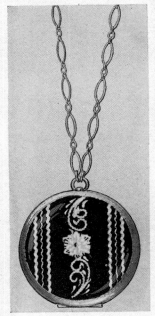

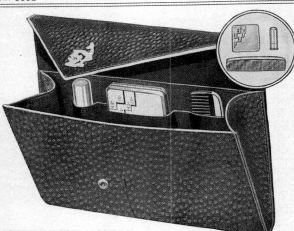

FRENCH ENAMELED OPERA COMPACT
Black French enameled front, with bright cut, hand engraved designs. Fine white gold filled locket, plain back. 24 inch chain. Contains full size powder cake, puff and non-breakable mirror.
No. 8650 Each................$3.75

FITTED UNDER ARM BAG
Genuine leather. Black Pelican grain piped with white. Contains change purse and thin model compact, non-tarnishing chromium finish, fitted with large mirror, patented Evans' Tap-Sift loose powder container and full size rouge. French Enamel front. Automatic swivel lipstick and pocket comb to match. Size 7½x5 inches.
No. 8653 Each.........$15.00
Enamel Color of Fittings: White

FRENCH ENAMELED OPERA COMPACT
Black enameled "Dancing Partners" on silver background, cream enameled border. Yellow gold filled locket, plain back, and 24 inch chain. Contains full size powder cake, puff and non-breakable mirror.
No. 8651 Each................$3.00

Enameled Opera Locket Compacts sold for between three and ten dollars. *The Fort Dearborn Gift Book*, 1932.

Pendant necklace/compacts with black enameled figural silhouettes, concealing mirror, powder and puff. They were originally called "Opera Locket Compacts." Easy to lift and open, one could take a quick and discreet check of make-up with these handy pieces. 1¾" x 1½". *The Curiosity Shop.* $150-225.

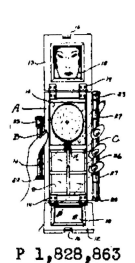

P 1,828,863

Oval enameled compact/pendant combination with pretty enameled and openworked neckchain. It opens to reveal metal mirror, powder, and puff. 1½" x 1". Shown with an enameled floral finger ring compact. 1" x ¾". *The Curiosity Shop.* Left, $175-225; right, $80-100.

Compact/belt buckle combinations were made, however, in low volumes. Although not as simple or discreet to use as the pendant or bracelet compact combination, they were available with a belt loop and hook on the reverse side, making it easily adaptable to a favorite belt strap. Ladies' hat pins were another rarity that contained compact tops. Tiny hinged hat pin heads would open to reveal a miniature powder compact with puff. They are desired by both compact and hat pin collectors.

Oriental motif silvered compact/ walking stick combination. Cane handle is a powder compact containing a mirror. Collar has ornamentation, mahogany or ebony wood shaft, metal ferrule protectors at tip of stick. 1¾" dia. *The Curiosity Shop*. $400-550.

Animal adorned objects have always been popular. Scottie dogs, elephants, monkeys, teddy bears, cats, dogs, and horse's heads adorned all sorts of knick knacks and compacts. There is a level of recognition that can help promote a sale of these pieces, whether a dog may resemble a beloved pet, or a horse head adorned compact could become a perfect gift for an equestrian enthusiast.

While Schuco made the furry miniature monkey and teddy bear compacts that conceal powder, puffs, and mirrors in their bellies and lipstick in their necks in the 1920s, it is unknown what company distributed the rare dog compact with floppy ears. A material used to resemble fur covers the body of the dog which is round and consists of powder and mirror. It has glass eyes and somber features, a red satin bow tied around its neck, and finishes with a fluffy dark tail. There is also a cat motif compact of which two versions are known to be in existence. One is a full-bodied cat, the other, just the face. Both are covered with fur-like material in a similar design to the dog compact. There are no markings on the cat compact.

Dog compact with floppy ears. A material used to resemble fur covers the round body of the dog which consists of powder and mirror. It has glass eyes and somber features, a red satin bow tied around its neck and finishes with a fluffy dark tail. 3" x 4½". *Lori Landgrebe Antiques*. Very rare.

Shown open to reveal mirror and compressed powder.

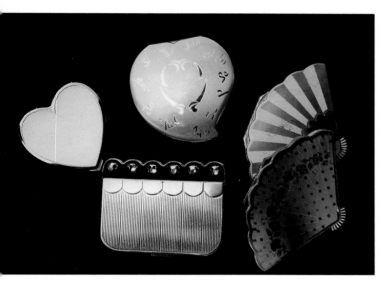

Left: heart shaped powder compact with heart shaped puff, 2½" x 3". Top: Elgin American stylized heart shaped compact with "Yes" and "I do" in different languages, 3¼" x 3¼". Right: two fan shaped compacts with varying goldtone designs, 3" x 3¼". Bottom: Coty "Sleigh Bells," goldtone case, puffs and case signed, mirror, circa: 1940s, 3" x 3¾". *The Curiosity Shop*. Left, $40-60; top center, $80-120; bottom center, $125-175; right, $60-80.

The star craze was started by the famous Italian designer Elsa Schiaparelli, who introduced dress clips in the shapes of metal stars and used star designs in other ways. Lamps, fabric, cigarette boxes, dressing table accessories, and waste paper baskets are only a few things that adopted this very simple, appealing design. Star shapes continued to be popular and carried over to designs later seen on the back of some Stratton compacts. Equally simple and delightful are heart shaped designs. Schiaparelli designed a rouge compact in a color she called "Rose S" which she introduced on her mannequins at her August showing in Paris in 1939. Heart and triangular shaped, they sold for about two dollars. In keeping with the revival of romanticism in the forties, heart shaped compacts of gilt or enamel made excellent gifts for sentimental occasions. Some can be found with engraved names or initials.

Compacts were considered novelties not only for what they resembled or the ensembles they matched, but also for what they did—and I don't mean just powdering a shiny nose! Those that played music when wound, or jingled when touched were quite a sensation. Let's look at the "Sleigh Bells" compact by Coty. Advertised as "a cheerful little eyeful and earful," six tiny bells located within a scalloped design at the top side of the compact tingled discreetly when moved. This compact was designed so that when held flat in the palm of one hand, fingers could comfortably wrap around the scalloped outer section holding the bells, and if practiced enough, one could open the compact with a thumb. This compact was launched in 1942 for five dollars along with the "Buckle," a sleek rectangular shaped compact with a goldtone belt buckle located on the top of the vanity. The buckle compact, invented by A.R. Botham, sold for $2.95 and was available in various enamel and/or goldtone combinations.

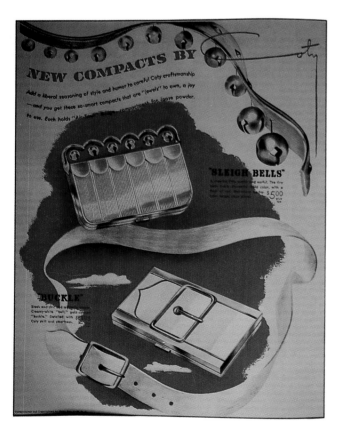

Coty "Sleigh Bells" and "Buckle." 1942.

Kigu "Flying Saucer" musical dome shaped compact with royal blue celestial scene on both sides. Plays the song "Some Enchanted Evening." 4" dia. *Author's Collection*. $350-450.

One of the most unusual figural compacts is the English Kigu "Flying Saucer" compact. If the fact that it is royal blue with a dome shaped celestial scene on both sides, taking on the appearance of a UFO is not enough to intrigue the buying public, consider the fact that it also plays "Some Enchanted Evening" when wound. The Saucer was also available without the musical playing mechanism. Carryalls, multi-compartmented, and mass-produced versions of the earlier minaudiere may be found with an interior musical box. While having ample space for cigarettes, they will sometimes come equipped with the popular old tune, "Smoke Gets in Your Eyes."

Compacts in the shapes of musical instruments are also a lot of fun to own. The Samaral tan leather guitar made in Spain is extremely detailed and was expensive to create. Strings adorn the neck along with gold plated brass bars and tuners. Inside, the sifter takes the shape of the guitar and leather trim finishes the outside hour glass shaped body of the compact. It opens on a hinge so that both the front and back of the leather adorned compact can be viewed simultaneously.

Silver drum shaped compacts with applied drum sticks on the lid and metal snares that appear to stretch from the bottom to the top rim, open to reveal a mirror and deep powder well.

Pygmalion designed a goldtone grand piano shaped compact with collapsible legs that was available either with or without a music box and a windup key located underneath. Interior puffs are stamped "Sonata" and lids were gilt or coated with mother-of-pearl. As part of the "Collector's Item" series, Volupté manufactured a metal compact with raised white and black enameled keys on a keyboard, made to resemble a legless grand piano.

Unorthodox items were depicted in the shapes of eight balls by Henriette, roulette wheels, dice topped domes, men's flannel shirts, hot air balloons, hands, guns, and sardine tins, to name just a few. Compacts in the shapes of castanets, vanity tables, purses, flower baskets, opera glasses, hand mirrors, and suitcases would seem to have a more sensible appeal to the compact buying public—namely women. But, this does not have an effect on current value today and can sometimes prove just the contrary.

Left: book shaped leather-like compact with rouge and powder, 2" x 3". Center: Volupté piano with enameled keys, 3" x 3". Right: two toned dome shaped globe, stamped "foreign" on the inside of the metal case, and Pygmalion on the powder puff, 2½" dia. *The Curiosity Shop.* Left, $75-100; center, $150-200; right, $250-350.

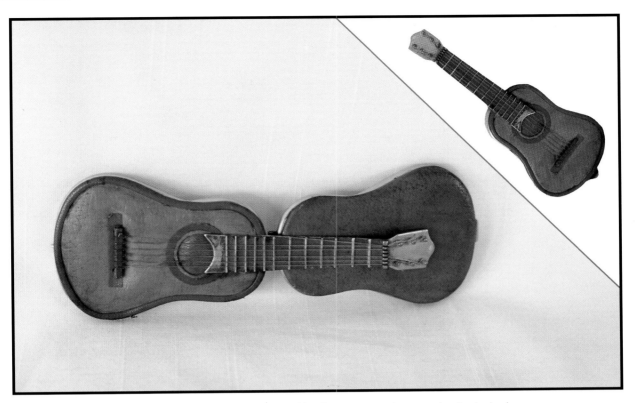

Shown open, Samaral leather guitar's the hour glass shaped body opens on a hinge so that both the front and back of the compact can be viewed simultaneously. Inside, the powder sifter takes the shape of the guitar. Details include plated brass ornamentation and strings. Spanish. 6". Rare. *Author's Collection.*

Top: Coty belt buckle motif with goldtone embossed lid, rouge and puffs, mirror, invented by A.R. Botham, it sold for $2.95. Circa: 1940s, 3¾" x 2¼". Bottom left: yellow enameled shell motif signed Elgin American with lip smudge, powder, puff, and mirror, 3" x 3". Bottom right: Cara Mia signed enameled clock case with moveable hands, mirror, powder puff, and sifter, larger mirror on underside. 3½" dia. *The Curiosity Shop.* Top, $80-125; bottom left, $75-95; bottom right, $60-90.

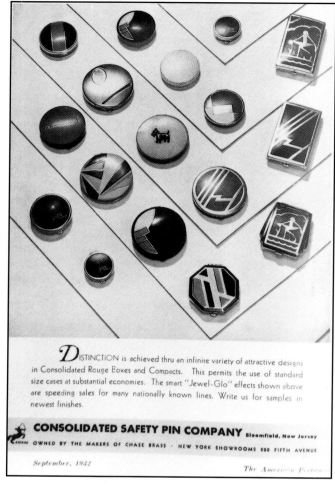

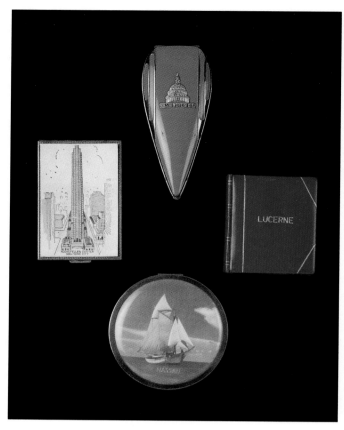

Compacts with Scotties and geometric shapes on lids were popular sellers in novelty stores. *The American Perfumer*, 1932.

Top: Washington, D.C., Art Deco inspired green enameled compact marked Elgin American, 4½" x 2". $75-125. Second row left: Rockefeller Center, New York City with enameled graphics marked Pilcher, 3½" x 2". $50-75. Right: Lucerne, Switzerland, red leather book shaped with gold trim, 3" x 2½". $80-100. Bottom: Nassau, Bahamas, a transfer made in England, 3" x 3¼". $50-75. *From the Collection of Joan Orlen, Photograph by Steven Freeman Photography.*

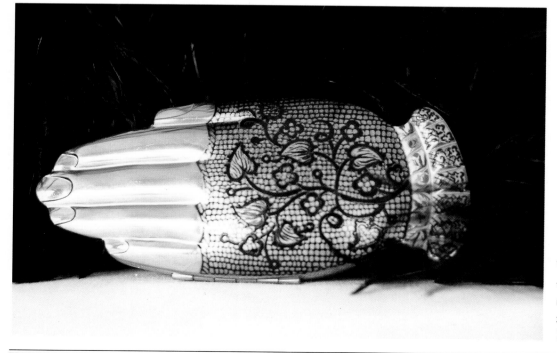

Volupté "Gay Nineties Mitt" with black lace. Advertised "to match a mischievous mood." 4½" x 2". *The Curiosity Shop*. $250-350.

Billiard Eight Ball by Henriette, black enameled loose powder compact with white enameled circle, faux ivory interior with mirror, shown with original box. Popular item in the vintage five and dime stores. 2" dia. *Author's Collection*. $150-200.

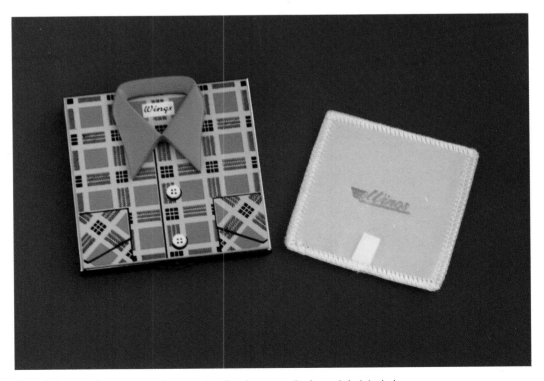

Flannel shirt motif compact with a raised collar that extends above lid. Made by Wadsworth, marked "Wings." Interior mirror reads "A Madison Creation." 3" x 3¼". *Lori Landgrebe Antiques*. Very rare.

"Balloon with Gondola," also called the "Hot Air Balloon." Goldtone loose powder vanity case with attached rouge pot. Faux ivory interior. 2" dia. *The Curiosity Shop*. Very rare.

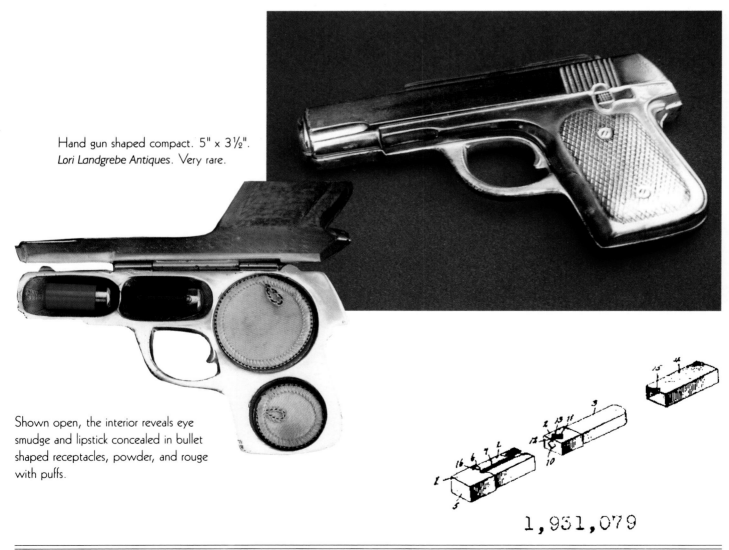

Hand gun shaped compact. 5" x 3½". *Lori Landgrebe Antiques*. Very rare.

Shown open, the interior reveals eye smudge and lipstick concealed in bullet shaped receptacles, powder, and rouge with puffs.

1,931,079

Brass ball shaped compact with pair of dice under plastic domed lid, shown with a non-regulation roulette wheel encased in plastic domed lid atop a gilded brass ball shaped compact. Both are 2" dia. and popular with those who collect gambling motif items as well as compact collectors. *The Curiosity Shop*. Left, $125-200; right, $225-275.

Unusual gray metal helmet conceals a compact. A jump ring pulls down on the bottom of the helmet to gain access to the hollow dome shaped receptacle used for powder. Interior puff has plastic jump ring attached. 1¾" x 2", 1 inch deep. *From the Collection of Joan Orlen, Photograph by Steven Freeman Photography*. Very rare.

French beret of black felt with colorful tassel top. 3" dia. Shown open to reveal mirror, sifter, and compartment for powder. Made in France. Rare. *Lori Landgrebe Antiques*.

Castanet shaped wooden compact with figural decal and Parisian insignia on reverse. Double silk tasseled carry cord with metal fittings. France. 4½" dia. *The Curiosity Shop*. $375-475.

Shown open to reveal mirror, puff, and sifter.

Givenchy gold plated clamshell compact with a blue faux jeweled thumbpiece. 3½" x 4". *The Curiosity Shop.* $100-150.

Flower basket motif compacts with rigid handles. Left: polished goldtone basket with painted flowers on the lid. Center: silk daisies enclosed in plastic domed lid. Right: floral basket with brightly colored lady bug encased under lid. *The Curiosity Shop.* Left, $125-175; center, $150-200; right, $150-200.

Top: dome shaped Henriette "Questioning Game Ball" with Yes/No/Maybe pockets and rolling ball under plastic lid, circa: 1941, 2" dia. Left: heart shaped powder compact with heart shaped puff, 2½" x 3". Right: black and white enameled eight ball dome shaped compact with powder well, 2½" x 3". *The Curiosity Shop.* Left, $40-60; top, $275-375; right, $150-200.

The American-made metal sardine can compact's case was manufactured by Hingeco Vanities, Inc., of Providence, Rhode Island. It is square with green enameling and a foreground of fashionable women in colorful costume. From Spain, Paris, London, Sweden, India, and New York, these models seem to radiate around the center of the compact which consists of an enameled globe. The only way to open this compact is to turn and pull the old-fashioned styled key, allowing the lid to spring open. Luckily, the key does not fully free itself from the compact or it would probably not be found intact today. A mirror, sifter, and powder are found inside.

Enameled sardine can compact with attached turn key. 4 x 4". *Author's Collection.* Very rare.

The metal sardine can compact's case was manufactured by Hingeco Vanities, Inc., of Providence, Rhode Island. *The American Perfumer,* 1931.

Ciner gilt and black enamel egg shaped minaudiere. The interior reveals a central mirror separating a powder compartment from an additional cubicle. Black enameled finger ring carrying chain. Extra heavy. 3" x 2" dia. Also shown: a thin Viennese enameled front with a green gold finish and finger ring attachment. Interior reveals mirror, loose powder compartment, sifter, and rouge. Sold wholesale for ten dollars in the 1930s. 2" dia. *The Curiosity Shop.* Left, $250-350; right, $125-175.

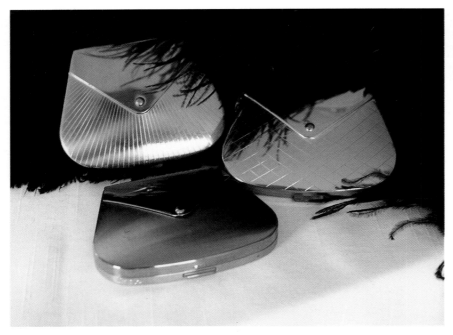

Voluptés "Lucky Purse," part of the Collector's Items series, available with several varying lid designs. *The Curiosity Shop.* $125-175 each.

Another American masterpiece, made by Wadsworth, is "The Operetta." Nestled in a rich, black satin fitted case that snaps closed, it is lined with hot pink satin and has a large mirror dominating the inside cover. These opera glasses have small, round, double mirrors where one would normally expect to find the lens. On the opposite side, where the eye pieces are located, is a pull out, twist-out, swansdown powder pli in one and in the other, a lipstick tube. Made of black plastic, this unusual compact combination has gold plated metal detailing around the lens pieces. It sold for about ten dollars in 1950.

."The Operetta" by Wadsworth. *Vogue*, 1950.

"The Operetta." Encased in a rich, black satin fitted case that snaps closed, these opera glasses have small round double mirrors where one would normally expect to find the lens. Made of black plastic, this unusual compact combination has gold plated metal detailing around the lens pieces. It sold for about ten dollars in 1950. 3" x 2½". *Author's Collection*. Very rare.

Shown open, it is evident that where the eye pieces are located is a pull out, twist-out swansdown powder pli and a lipstick tube. The fitted black satin case is lined with hot pink satin and has a large mirror dominating the inside cover.

The "Eversmart Manicure Compact" was patented in December 1924. Combining one grooming aspect with another, this unique combination was made by The Wahl Company in Chicago, who manufactured Eversharp Pencils and Wahl Pens. Of clever design and ingenious construction, it was practical and small. On opposite ends of the goldtone metal cylinder are two small dispensers, one that twists to distribute powder, the other a pli. Less than three inches in length, it took less space in the purse than a regular powder compact and kept all manicure parts secured. The other parts of the compact include: a buffer with chamois, nail file, emery board, manicure stick, nail white, and polish. The company guaranteed to replace all parts that wore out,

and orders were taken for refills. Priced reasonably, a complete refill of all parts would cost one dollar.

Voluptés unadorned gilt metal or brushed gold hand shaped compacts were originally called the "The Golden Gesture" in 1946 and were inspired by the art of the East. In 1948, the same compact, decorated with an enameled white or black lace glove, was called the "Gay Nineties Mitt." The mitt was designed by the company "to reflect the prettiest faces and match a mischievous mood." This compact was also available with a faux diamond engagement ring (a great gift for a bridal shower), a faux diamond bracelet, and a manicured fingernail version. These compacts sold for between five and thirty dollars.

Patented in December 1924. Combining one grooming aspect with another, this unique combination was made by the Wahl Company in Chicago. The "Eversmart Manicure Compact" shown open to reveal on opposite ends of the goldtone metal cylinder are two small dispensers, one that twists to distribute powder, the other a pli. Parts of the compact include a buffer with chamois, nail file, emery board, manicure stick, nail white, and polish. A complete refill of all parts would cost one dollar. 3". *The Curiosity Shop.* $200-300.

P 1,836,722

Vintage Compacts & Beauty Accessories

Regional souvenir compacts. First row left: Niagara Falls, painted, 3½" x 3½". $40-60. Right: Kentucky Derby Louisville, Kentucky, by Zell, wooden case, Bakelite lid, 4½" dia. $125-175. Second row left: Scottsman, hand painted bag pipe player with castle in background, made in Great Britain, 3" dia. $40-60. Center: Mardi Gras, New Orleans, leather pouch bottom, loose powder, 2½" dia. $75-100. Right: London souvenir, enameled by Vogue vanities, made in England, 4" dia. $75-125. Bottom left: "Elk on the Trail," Mohawk Trail, Massachusetts, transfer on enamel, rouge and powder interior, 2½" x 1¾". $30-60. Center: Niagara Falls in oval, hand painted with jewels, marked "Jolie amour poudre," 2" x 3". $50-75. Right: camera shaped by Girey of Miami, Florida, 3½" x 1¾". $80-100. *From the Collection of Joan Orlen, Photograph by Steven Freeman Photography.*

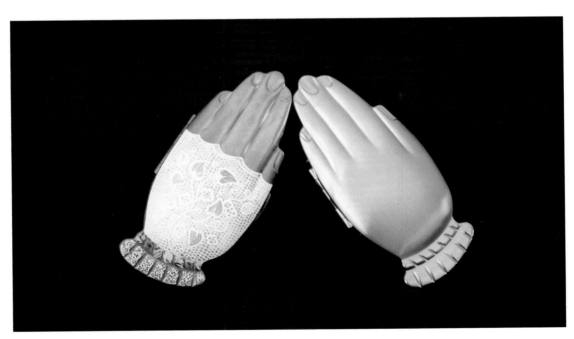

Gay Nineties Mitt by Volupté with white lace and the Golden Gesture. Both are 4½" x 2". *The Curiosity Shop.* Left, $250-350; right, $175-225.

Suitcase shaped compacts were very well received gift ideas in the popular five and dime novelty stores. A variety of manufacturers made a selection of different types and designs of suitcases, including the English Kigu and American Atomette. Some were available with travel stickers from Rome, Cuba, New York, Paris, and all sorts of exotic locations. These labels were hand applied and positioned in various areas at the whim of the designer. Many suitcases had rigid metal handles. Some were embellished with a leather looking exterior, while others had been paid great attention to, with enameling and gilt metal fittings made to look like suitcase straps.

Volupté created a beautiful scalloped edged compact designed to resemble a vanity table with collapsible legs. Called the "Petite Boudoir," it was a perfect miniature of the carved golden dressing table that Marie Antoinette used and loved in her own bed chamber. Distributed in 1950, it was included in the series of Volupté's "Collector's Items." Wadsworth distributed a vanity table that was rectangular. It also had collapsible legs and was advertised in the same year.

Zell created a flower basket with an attractive scalloped design cut out of metal. It has a rigid metal handle and was available with or without pearls adorning the front. Usually, the compact has traces of very light pastel tinting. The Zell basket is made so that it can stand freely by the bottom rim of the basket.

Red enameled and gilt vanity case designed to resemble a suitcase, artistically decorated with travel stickers. 3" x 2½". *From the Collection of Kay Miguez, Photograph by Miguez Photography.* $250-350.

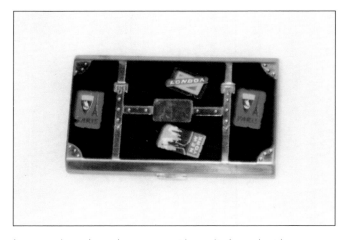

Luggage shaped metal compact with applied travel stickers. 2" x 3½". *The Curiosity Shop.* $200-275.

"Atomette" suitcase shaped store stock compacts in original pink polka-dot boxes with felt sleeves. Covered front and back with leather-like material or rich green textured fabric. Made in Great Britain, each measures 2½" x 3". *The Curiosity Shop.* $150-225 each.

Volupté Petite Boudoir, designed to resemble a vanity table with collapsible legs. "A perfect miniature of the carved golden dressing table Marie Antoinette loved in her boudoir." Also shown open. Included in Volupté's series of Collector's Items in the early fifties. 3" x 2¼". *The Curiosity Shop*. $275-375.

Made in France, this black suede camera shaped vanity unsnaps to open accordion style to gain access into a purse. The top left is a lipstick, interior reveals a round mirror, compact, and sifter. 4" x 7". *From the Collection of Joan Orlen, Photograph by Steven Freeman Photography*. Rare.

Many childhood novelty compacts were very popular and are now very collectible. For instance, the "Three Little Pigs" were depicted on a charming novelty compact in the 1930s. The "Big Bad Wolf" also went to market on his own compact, but because of his un-savory reputation, he was consider-ably less popular with the public than the charming pig trio. This helps to demonstrate the point that with whim-sical and figural compacts, it is impor-tant what design is chosen. On the flip side, what may have been con-sidered a failure then, financial or oth-erwise, is often a formula for reversed opinion today. Just imagine for a mo-ment, how collectible the "Wolf" compact, dress clip, or sardine com-pact is today, none of which were exactly block buster sellers at the time. Largely, for financial reasons, manufac-turers kept abreast of trends when these novelty compacts were made, and when it was dis-covered that they were not selling as quickly as they would have liked, they were eliminated from the market. Coupling this with the reduced likelihood that a compact like the Big Bad Wolf was treasured and saved makes the compact much less prone to be found today and desirability runs higher.

Famous faces and other nursery rhyme characters also adorned compact covers. Shirley Temple, Little Bo Peep, Charlie McCarthy, and Scarlett O'Hara joined the ranks of easily familiar subjects. Charlie McCarthy's compact was a mesh bottomed vanity pouch with a raised McCarthy head on black enamel by Evans. His likeness could also be found on a square compact with the raised head on the lid. Relying on recognition to promote sales, Shirley Temple was not only depicted on a leather-like compact during her child-hood, but was also, much later, commissioned to be a spokes-person for the Coronation Carryall by the Evans Case Com-pany while she starred in *The Story of Seabiscuit* by Warner Brothers in 1949. This carryall was fitted with a pop-up lipstick, covered powder well, puff, comb, and coin holder with a separate space for cigarettes, hanky, or keys. The lid is adorned with a faux jeweled crown in an oval medallion.

In the late forties, Rita Hayworth was hired by Volupté to promote the "Lucky Purse" during the time that she starred in the Columbia motion picture, *Carmen*. This compact, a part of Volupté's "Collector's Items" series, was in the shape

Little Bo Peep. 2" dia.
The Curiosity Shop. $75-150.

of a purse and came with a textured, brushed gold finish, a smooth gilt finish, and with other details, including a wrist chain made to resemble a purse strap.

The Scarlett O'Hara compact, featured in the movie press book for the M.G.M. film *Gone With the Wind* sold for two dollars at department and novelty stores. There were three styles cre-ated in 1940, all Southern scenes taking inspiration from the epic film. This compact is sought after by both compact collectors and *Gone With the Wind* enthusiasts.

In 1949, The Elgin American Company launched a slew of square brushed goldtone compacts with colorful caricatures and verses based on popular Zodiac concepts. Pack-aged in gift boxes, they came equipped with an interior beveled mirror, puff, and powder well.

Novelty compacts, during these times, were packed with surprise and freshness, but for business purposes they were continually changed to keep pace with the fickle moods and fancies of the buying public.

Shirley Temple motif compact with red leather-like cover. 4" x 4".
Lori Landgrebe Antiques. $125-175.

Advertising lipstick for "Gibson's" whiskey, shown with unsigned powder compact with woman and fan. 3" dia. *The Curiosity Shop*. Top, $40-60; bottom, $35-65.

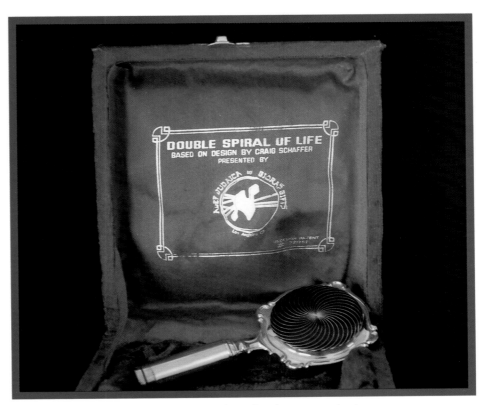

Black and goldtone swirled compact shaped as a hand mirror in red velvet presentation box. Called the "Double Spiral of Life," it was designed by Craig Schaffer. Lipstick is concealed in the handle, interior and exterior contain beveled glass mirrors. 2½" x 5¼". *The Curiosity Shop*. $125-175.

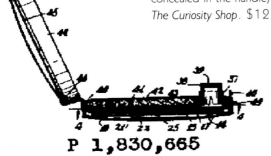

P 1,830,665

Evans pink and goldtone heart shaped basketweave compact. Circa: 1946. 4" x 4". *The Curiosity Shop*. $145-185.

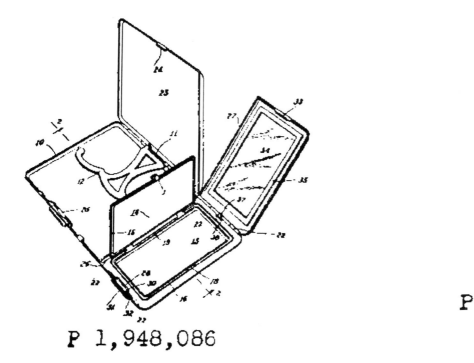

P 1,948,086

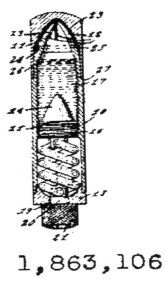

P 1,863,106

Chapter Four
Compact & Vanity Purses

Vanity purses, also known as compact purses, are purses with a compact appurtenance either incorporated into the frame or attached to a purse in a unique way. They are a novelty, a unique combination of two items, and have a double level of collectibility, desirable of both compact and purse enthusiasts. Advanced compact collectors may collect vanity purses and this sometimes helps to bridge the gap between compact and purse collecting. Many a serious compact purse devotee has evolved into an ardent purse collector.

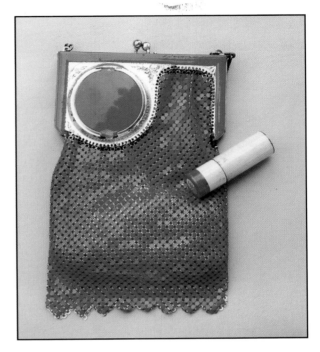

Different vanity purse designs find the compact portion in various locations. This unusual Whiting and Davis Company "Corner Compact Costume Bag" has a front side compact incorporated into the red enameled frame. The interior of compact reveals a metal mirror, rouge, powder, and puffs with a lined enameled mesh purse. Shown with a Richard Hudnut lipstick. 4" x 6½". *The Curiosity Shop*. $500-800.

BE WITH YOU IN A MINUTE

© REINTHAL & NEWMAN PUBS. N Y

Vanity purses are a challenge to collect and are especially entertaining when inventive designs find the compact portion of the purse in different locations. For instance, it could be centered or to the left of the frame, visible from the front of the purse. Or, it can be situated on the top or the center of the purse with only the side of the compact visible when held upright.

Many such purses were intended for late afternoon or evening wear by discriminating well-dressed women. They are usually, but not always, part mesh and manufactured in the 1920s and 1930s. Some were composed entirely of early plastics such as Bakelite or celluloid. Others were cloth with frames of brass or plated metals. There are also those made entirely of metal or sterling such as the *necessaire* which

The R&G Company vanity purse with sterling enameled floral lid and finely crafted foxtail wrist strap. High quality embossing surrounds the metal bands containing the compact which is clearly visible from the top of the purse. 2½" x 7". *From the Collection of Joyce Morgan, Photograph by Harry Barth.* $500-700.

From the Collection of Joyce Morgan, Photograph by Harry Barth. $350-450.

is a small bolster shaped combination of compact and purse or the exquisite sterling and enameled bolster shaped vanity purse with lipstick and fringe, manufactured by F & B. Some of the companies that manufactured vanity purses include: Whiting & Davis, F & B, Evans, Bliss-Napier, and R & G.

Theodore W. Foster & Brothers Company were manufacturing jewelers and silversmiths, producing a beautiful selection of dresser sets, fobs, lorgnettes, jewelry, hand purse mirrors, perfume holders, vanity purses, and powder compacts. They began business in 1873 with the main office and factory located in Providence, Rhode Island. Their quality workmanship, which included compacts of sterling silver, brocaded, engine turned, enameled, gilt finished and gold filled, quickly led to expansion of offices in New York City, Chicago, and Los Angeles. Known for their high quality and attention to detail, their registered trademark consisted of a flag with the letters "F & B."

Many vanity purses were intended for late afternoon or evening wear by discriminating well dressed women.

Vintage Compacts & Beauty Accessories

The *Necessaire*, a sterling silver bolster shaped vanity purse that encases a compact under the lid. 1¾" x 4". *From the Collection of Joyce Morgan, Photograph by Harry Barth*. Rare.

The F&B sterling vanity purse was available in orange and ivory with refills for powder, rouge, and lipstick. *The Foster Blue Book*, 1925.

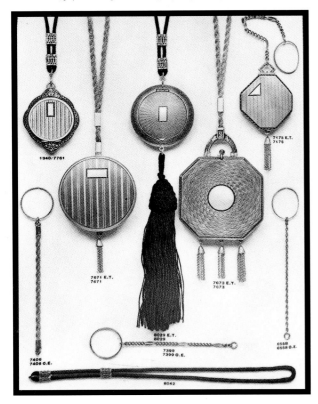

F&B vanity cases with fancy tassels and carry chains. *The Foster Blue Book*, 1925-26.

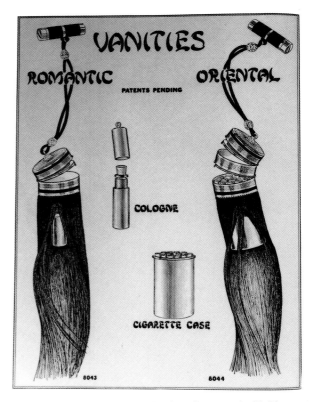

The Theodore W. Foster & Brother Company's (F&B) vanity purses. The *Romantic* has a compact top with a cologne vial bottom. The *Oriental* has a larger bottom that could be used for cigarettes. Both have black carry cords that attach to lipsticks and long tasseled bottoms. *The Foster Blue Book*, 1925.

F&B powder compacts. *The Foster Blue Book*, 1925-26.

Napier/Bliss. *Courtesy of The Napier Company archives*, 1921.

With a large selection of quality goods to offer, salespeople could not carry samples of all the company's work. As a result, in the first quarter of the century a detailed catalog called the *Foster Blue Book* was offered, showcasing goods with an thorough, illustrated color section for the enameled compact and vanity purse line. In it were presented a large selection of fine quality compacts and vanity purses, many of sterling and enamel, with the more elaborate selling for up to ninety dollars. Refills for powders were offered at a small additional cost. Compacts could be purchased with or without a tango chain (a chain, usually linked, that connects a compact with a lipstick) and finger ring (a chain that attaches a compact to a ring that can be worn on the finger).

An outstanding piece of workmanship made by this manufacturer is the bolster shaped sterling silver vanity purse with an enameled top in various colors, including red, green, tur-

quoise, orchid, orange, and ivory. This vanity has an engine turned cover with two black enameled lines. When the lid is opened, the interior has a compartment for powder and puff on the bottom and rouge and puff on the underside of the lid. There is a double swinging mirror, and some have been furnished with a memo tablet. The small cologne vial holder or larger cigarette case is concealed by long silk fringe in a color that corresponds with the enameling on the lid. The cologne vial vanity purse was called the Romantic; the cigarette holder, the Oriental. Lipstick holders were usually enameled black and attached on the end of a black silk adjustable wrist cord, decorated with gilt filigree ball slides. Refills for lipsticks, powders, and rouge, along with sifters allowing the customer to use her favorite choice of loose powder were also offered. These vanities originally sold wholesale for fifty to sixty dollars. Today, they are extremely hard to find and are very collectible.

The Bliss/Napier Company was founded in 1875 when a Mr. Whitney and a Mr. Rice rented a small amount of space in North Attleboro, Massachusetts, to manufacture men's watch chains and small gifts including compacts and vanity purses. Sales Agent Edgerton Ames Bliss and a Mr. Carpenter agreed on a great future for jewelry and novelties, so they purchased the company in 1882 and changed the company's name to Carpenter and Bliss. Soon, it was evident that thirty-three year old Bliss was becoming the active head of the fledgling company. In July of that year, Carpenter retired and the company was incorporated as the E.A. Bliss Company. With a larger offering of goods and a New York office, Bliss, originally from New York State, traveled extensively to Europe to keep current on Parisian fashions. There he purchased stones and beads used to accentuate compacts, purse frames, and manufacture jewelry. The company owed much of its early success to his untiring efforts.

Artist's rendering of ornate vanity case designed for Bliss, circa: 1910. *Courtesy of The Napier Company archives.*

In 1893, Bliss moved the main factory to an old ivy covered brick flint glass factory in Meriden, Connecticut, that was one of the first ornamental glass producing plants in the country. Bliss hired William R. Rettenmeyer as the new chief designer and stylist, who brought to his credit an apprenticeship in silversmithing at the renowned Tiffany and Company.

E.A. Bliss was the first to manufacture sterling silver giftware, compacts, and novelties in Meriden. Eventually, the city became known as *the silver city* throughout the world, and The E.A. Bliss Company was considered one of the most prosperous in the area. Their product line was varied with jewelry and giftware, including: match safes, sterling silver bonnet brushes, silver buckles, ornate manicure and stationary articles, fancy handled shoe horns and buttonhooks, sterling lorgnettes, elaborate silver trays, compacts, vanity purses, and lovely chatelaine purses. Launching an advertising campaign to reach quality retailers, they became a large supplier to fine jewelry and department stores. The fashion jewelry and accessories they offered grew in favor with the well-dressed gentlemen and ladies of the day. In the early 1900s, the New York office was moved to busy Fifth Avenue. Rettenmeyer's son Frederick joined the company in 1907. The company trademark during these early years consisted of "EA Co" in script with an imprint of a bee in flight above the letters, set inside a circle.

Chatelaine hooks of various designs were produced to coincide with a selection of adornment fittings that could include vinaigrettes (a glass lined conceit that held aromatic vinegar, smelling salts, and the like), scissors, bon bons (an ornamental flower or heart shaped locket), writing tablets, combs, compacts, and small purses. Chatelaine purses and handkerchief pockets were of ring or armor plate mesh made from a variety of materials, including white metal, gun metal, silver, and nickel silver. Many were lined with kid leather. Finishes on purse frames included French grey burnished, old silver, and imitation gun metal. Mesh could be had in quadruple plate, silver, gun metal, or glazed in Roman gold, bright silver, satin, or old silver. Ornate fittings could also be purchased separately. The wholesale

cost of single chatelaine purses ranged from eighteen to forty-two dollars each. Bon bons were sold by the dozen for about ten dollars.

In 1911, at sixty-two years of age, Edgerton Bliss died suddenly. Active in the company until the time of his death, he had spent the greater part of his life devoted to the development of the company bearing his name. His son, William E. Bliss, who was vice president of the company, became the active head soon after his father's death.

For a few short years beginning in 1911, exceptional designs of compacts were created with intent for production at Bliss. Unsigned by the originator, they were created on a special type of thin waxed paper that had been folded in half before being drawn to assure symmetry. Sketched, then tipped in color, they showed glorious detail incorporating gemstones, enameling, innovative shapes, and originality. Some of the compact designs included descriptive information such as "vanity case." It is not known whether these unique pieces of artwork were made by the famed Tiffany apprentice, Mr. Rettenmeyer, who was employed at Bliss during this time. While a shroud of mystery still surrounds these rare pieces discovered in Napier Company archives, it remains unknown whether these designs were manufactured or exist solely as archival drafts. Bliss must have foreseen their importance. Many were found precisely dated with red ink and stamped: "Received, Repair Department," or simply, "E.A. Bliss."

In the winter of 1913, William Rettenmeyer retired as head of the design department and his son, Frederick took over his responsibilities. A year later, James H. Napier was hired as General Manager and Director. Under his direction, the company was revitalized with new personnel, machinery, and products. Promotions and advertisements were increased as Napier instigated an immense period of development.

In 1919, the company introduced a fine mesh purse called *Nile-Gold* that was available with variations in the frame design including one that attached to a compact. By advertising it in the trade publication, they could reach retail distributors who purchased in quantity. They also advertised in national publications like *Vogue* and *The Red Book*. Bliss mesh purses included a complimentary silk pouch to be used in place of a lining. Along with the pouch came directions for the care of the vanity purse with instructions for submitting it for repair service if needed.

The company trademark was changed again, this time to a rectangle shape with the word "Bliss" inside. In 1920, Napier was elected President and General Manager. In recognition of his work in the growth and revitalization of the business, the name of the company was changed to The Napier-Bliss Company.

In the spring of 1921, the company introduced a vanity purse called the *Du Barry Purse*. It has a lovely embossed, arched frame in the shape of an inverted "V," fine mesh body, metal fringed tassel, and an artistically carved powder case. Innovative designs like this one, used to incorporate the compact into the purse design in new ways, are a delight to find. The company attached the compact not into the frame, as was most often done, but instead to the braided mesh carry strap. When not in use, the finely detailed powder case lay in the hand when the purse was carried. The company promoted it as "the perfect combination mesh purse and powder box, for the woman who appreciates the value of correct dress accessories" with advertisements depicting a woman holding the purse and, simultaneously, using the powder case with ease. The *Du Barry* was first introduced to the jewelry industry through a formal announcement in *The Jewelers' Circular* trade publication. After the initial introduction, it was advertised in *Vogue* to reach the retail buyer. It was available in 14 karat green gold, gold filled, sterling, and the company's innovation: *Nile-Gold*. The purse was sold through fine quality jewelry stores and, if found today, will have "Bliss" stamped into the frame.

Napier's contribution to the company was once again rewarded when the business name was changed to The Napier Company. During the 1920s, The Napier Company manufactured another unique vanity purse that incorporated the powder box in a similar fashion to the *Du Barry*. It also had a powder box attached at the end of a braided mesh carry chain with a fine mesh purse body. The design on the purse frame was a pretty, graduated scallop, and instead of a single tasseled finish, this purse finished in chain fringe. It was advertised in a trade publication along with another new tango chain vanity case. If found today, this vanity purse would have "Napier" stamped into the frame. Both of these vanity purses sold so well, along with their other successful lines, that in 1928 land and a large building on Cambridge Street in Meriden, Connecticut, was purchased and became known as Napier Park.

In the early 1940s, The Napier Company transformed its facilities to manufacture war materials. Among other items, radar panels, medals, metal bushings, and millions of identification tags were produced. Highly skilled in precision work, brilliant designers and engineers developed a new process that conserved precious bronze at a time when metal supplies were critically low. Military items temporarily replaced jewelry, purses, and accessories on factory floors.

Over the years, The Napier Company continued to grow, opening sales offices in Chicago, Texas, and Los Angeles. In 1960, James Napier died and Frederick Rettenmeyer was elected president. In the mid-eighties, representatives continued in the tradition set by Bliss by making European trips to purchase goods. The Napier Company continues to the present day.

The Wade Davis Company, founded in 1876 in Plainville, Massachusetts, was owned by William H. Wade and Edward P. Davis. In 1880, one of the company office helpers was an ambitious teenager named Charles A. Whiting. Due to his enthusiasm and determination, this energetic young man was steadily promoted from his nine cents per hour office position to New York sales manager. Remarkably, he became a partner in the company while still in his twenties. Sixteen years later in 1896, he and Edward P. Davis formed a partnership and raised enough capital to purchase the company. Together, they changed the name to The Whiting & Davis Company and introduced the famous mesh purses and eventually, vanity purses. In 1907, Whiting purchased Davis's interest in the company and became President and Treasurer. He incorporated the business, and in a grand gesture, chose to continue with the name of the prospering company as a tribute to his longtime loyal partner.

An *El-Sah* vanity purse, a floral enameled motif decorates the compact lid. 3½" x 7½". *From the Collection of Joyce Morgan, Photograph by Harry Barth.* $375-475.

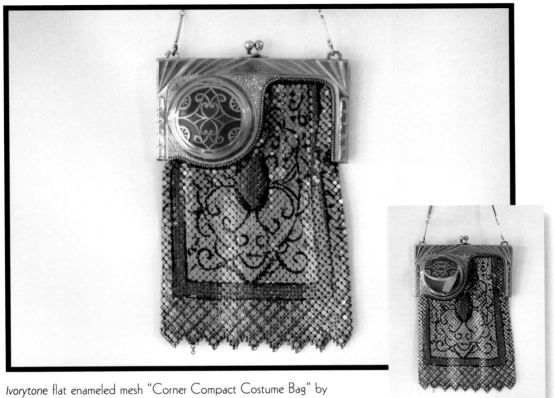

Ivorytone flat enameled mesh "Corner Compact Costume Bag" by Whiting and Davis. The enameled compact is attached to the frame on the side of the front. 4½" x 6½". *The Curiosity Shop.* $500-800.

The compact shown open.

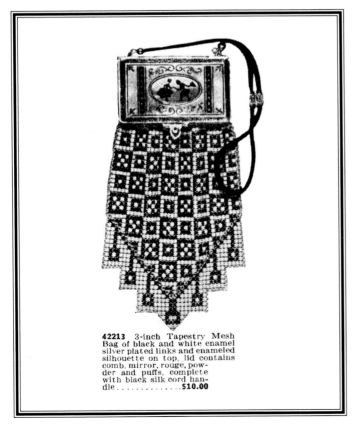

42213 3-inch Tapestry Mesh Bag of black and white enamel silver plated links and enameled silhouette on top, lid contains comb, mirror, rouge, powder and puffs, complete with black silk cord handle............**$10.00**

George T. Brodnax, Inc., 1926.

Whiting and Davis baby fine mesh vanity purse in goldtone. 3½" x 7½". *The Curiosity Shop.* $375-475.

Demand for the mesh purses the company produced was steadily increasing. Made by hand, the work was meticulous. Whiting was acutely aware that a finished product ready for the marketplace took valuable time, so he was eager to establish a faster, more efficient method of manufacturing the mesh. Accordingly, in 1912 he sought the aid of A.C. Pratt, the inventor of the world's first automatic mesh machine. Whiting & Davis became the first company to use automatic mesh making machineries that were soon rendered their exclusive property as they became the holders of the mesh making patents. The new reliable machinery increased the production of mesh purses tremendously. In conjunction with the growing volume, the company launched a major nationwide advertising campaign and soon became the world's leading mesh manufacturer.

Aiming to reach the average family, and now able to keep costs down by producing in quantity, the company was capable of creating a fast selling, affordable product. Year round advertising was intensified close to graduation, Mother's Day, and the holiday seasons.

By 1922, the Whiting & Davis Company had a branch factory in Quebec, Canada, a New York office on Fifth Avenue, and a Chicago branch in addition to their factory headquarters in Massachusetts. Their staff of fifty expert engineers and mechanics developed and registered numerous additional patents and constructed nearly all the special machines used to make mesh right in their plants. The firm was the first to use solder-filled wire in making metal mesh. Three hundred and fifty highly automated mesh making machines were operating. A busy maze of machinery spun bars of solid metal into threads of gold and silver that were woven into many patterns and shapes of mesh. If ever a single link was missed, or if the end of the spooled wire was reached, the machine automatically stopped until an attendant, who was in charge of up to fifteen machines at once, could remedy the problem.

A finished vanity purse might contain 100,000 links, each soldered individually. When the mesh was placed in an electric furnace, the thin trace of solder in each link melted

and flowed. Usage of a fine spiral wire to join the mesh body to the frame was a method the company introduced to improve the previously inferior process of connecting with separate links. At first, the purses were joined to their frames with separate delicate links which were weakened when they were spread open. Later, the company introduced a fine spiral wire to join the mesh body to the frame. This procedure can be seen where the compact/frame of most vanity purses is attached to the mesh bottom. With the new spiral wire process one end could be freed and the whole spiral removed easily without opening a single link. This innovative method was called *hanging up*. A *mesh to the edge* feature was another Whiting & Davis innovation that gave a smooth silhouette at the hinges, and thereby added to the artistry of the purse. The Whiting & Davis logo was impressed into the metal compact purse frame and/or attached, with a small hanging metal tag, on the interior of the purse.

Fabulous vanity purses of enameled flat mesh, also known as Armor Mesh, were offered in varied colors and when put into unusual patterns, the purses were well received. Single tiles or links were sometimes referred to as the *spider*. Links used to make the flat mesh purse consisted of a small piece of flat metal plate in the shape of a diamond with tiny "arms" at each point. The arms connected with a small metal ring at each corner in order to create a flat surface. High speed presses punched out a large number of links and rings. They were individually woven into long sleeves of mesh fabric, then cut and sized.

Whiting & Davis guaranteed their purses' durability and dependability, and supported their fine workmanship by establishing a well-maintained service department, located in a special section of the plant. Under expert supervision, the department was a miniature factory in itself. No matter how roughly a purse was used, there was never a time when one could not be made as good as new either without charge or for a small fraction of the original cost. In the service department, purses were taken apart and completely renewed. They were washed, polished, and could even be replated if

Vintage Compacts & Beauty Accessories

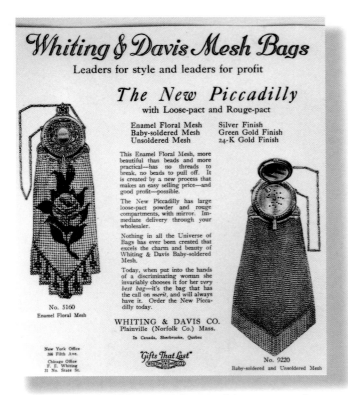

The *New Piccadilly* by Whiting and Davis with loose-pact and rouge-pact. *Courtesy of The Napier Company archives.*

were given names such as Venetian, Egyptian, and Bacchus. Especially ornate was the Venetian design that had a flared insert just above the fringe. In this decade, too, the free flowing lines that emulated drapes of Classic Greek clothing were brought into vogue by The Whiting & Davis Company as they adapted these styles into mesh purse production.

Whiting & Davis mesh vanity purses were made in a constant parade of new patterns. Company representatives kept a non-stop vigil on the world of fashion in Paris and New York, enabling the company to anticipate major movements in the ever-changing modes of fashion.

Many ingenious vanity purses were introduced by The Whiting & Davis Company whose slogans included: "Hand in hand with fashion," and "Gifts that last." The *Delysia* is

necessary. Hinges on vanity purses were replaced and ball socket closures were resoldered. The company generously offered to repair other American made mesh purses for a moderate fee. When they were reassembled to original specifications, usually within two to three weeks, they were sent back to their owners. It is intriguing to think that some of the existing purses may have been reconditioned by the specialists at Whiting & Davis.

Some of the styles of Whiting & Davis soldered and unsoldered mesh offered included: Fine Ring Mesh (also known as Baby Ring Mesh), Sunset Mesh, and Fishscale Mesh. Sunset Mesh was available in various color combinations such as eighteen karat gold plate and silver plate in alternating gold, bronze, and brass stripes. Fishscale Mesh was made from a flat linked mesh with an attractive sheen.

Vanity purses early in the twentieth century were made of sterling silver, 14 karat gold, 18 karat gold plate, and silver plate, and had a fine, silky texture, an almost liquid suppleness. Since these purses did not have colored enamel, alluring designs were created with variations in frame shapes, locations of compacts, and embossing with linked carry chains and mesh straps, and a variety of unusual fringe designs that

The *Delysia* was manufactured by The Whiting and Davis Company in the 1920s in standard, junior, and petite sizes. 2" x 4". $500-750.

Inset: Shown open, the compact portion of the *Delysia* is revealed. 2" x 4". *From the Collection of Paula Higgins.*

arguably the most unique vanity purse that this company made, and is without question highly desirable today. The compact portion of this purse is encased in metal bands in the center, rather than the more customary positioning in the frame at the top. A pocket of mesh is found on the top and on the bottom of the purse where it is adorned with a tassel. Carry strap positioning is at the top center of the purse, attached to a metal reinforcement cap that was artfully crafted and etched. Frame bands that encompass the center of the purse have fine detailing. A *Delysia* featured in *Cosmopolitan* in December 1924 contained two mirrors, and a powder and rouge compact. It was made in gold, silver, sunset mesh, and what was promoted as "colored tapestry mesh," (a unique way to advertise enameling). Whiting & Davis called the *Delysia* the "utility mesh purse." This purse was sold at prestigious jewelry stores and could also be found in jewelry departments at fine stores in prices ranging from five to five hundred dollars.

Also introduced was the *Baby Peggy* that came in gold, silver, or enameled mesh and was meant for "her" daughter. Although this purse was not a genuine vanity purse, as it did not include a compact, it is worth mentioning since it was fashioned after the *Delysia*. The bottom of the purse is mesh but the top is silk. It could be drawn to a close with a pull cord instead of the mesh capped adult version that had a carry strap. The manufacturer cleverly described it as "grown up in every way but in price." This variation helped to keep the manufacturing cost low while still maintaining the general appearance of the *Delysia*.

The *Piccadilly* was a popular vanity purse made in the twenties in which a round compact was incorporated into the frame at the top of the purse. The bodies of these purses were usually made with fine ring or baby soldered mesh, but one of the few exceptions was the *New Piccadilly* which had a large rose and foliage enameled onto the armor mesh links. It contained soft powder and rouge with sifters referred to as "loose-pact" and "rouge-pact."

The *El-Sah* vanity purse has a rectangular shaped compact as part of the frame. Compact lids were enameled in floral designs, jeweled, or with a black silhouetted scene of a man and woman in a dance pose. If the compact is contained within the frame of the purse in this fashion, access to the compact portion is gained when the thumbpiece is depressed and the lid is lifted up. Inside, the compact top has an oval mirror and a clip to hold a comb. The jewel and enamel crested *El-Sah* has an additional metal plate that separates the powder from a calling card holder. On the bottom

Blue and white enameled mesh *Delysia*. The compact is centrally located. 3" x 6". *From the Collection of Joyce Morgan, Photograph by Harry Barth.* $500-750.

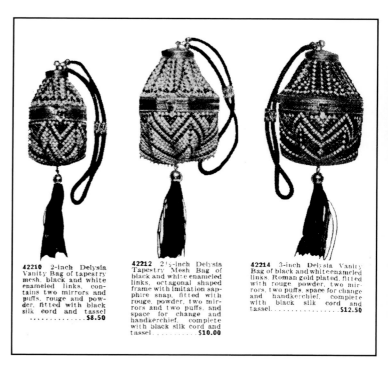

42210 2-inch Delysia Vanity Bag of tapestry mesh, black and white enameled links, contains two mirrors and puffs, rouge and powder, fitted with black silk cord and tassel $8.50

42212 2½-inch Delysia Tapestry Mesh Bag of black and white enameled links, octagonal shaped frame with imitation sapphire snap, fitted with rouge, powder, two mirrors and two puffs, and space for change and handkerchief, complete with black silk cord and tassel $10.00

42214 3-inch Delysia Vanity Bag of black and white enameled links Roman gold plated, fitted with rouge powder, two mirrors, two puffs, space for change and handkerchief, complete with black silk cord and tassel..................$12.50

George T. Brodnax, Inc., 1926.

Left: The *Piccadilly* by Whiting and Davis with compact portion centered on wishbone shaped frame, goldtone fine soldered mesh body, adjustable wrist strap, powder well, puff, and mirror. 3" x 7". Right: Evans goldtone flat mesh vanity purse. Interior reveals powder, mirror, and puff. 4" x 6". *The Curiosity Shop.* Left, $150-200; right, $125-175.

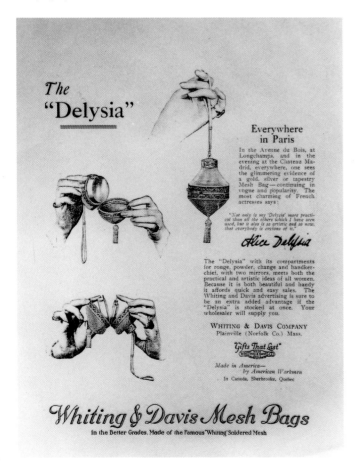

The *Delysia* shown open to reveal center compact. *Courtesy of The Napier Company archives.*

are two pots, holding compressed powder and rouge with individual silk lined puffs. Entrance to the purse portion is attained by lifting the entire compact section. Here, there is room for some small items such as money, a hanky, and other trinkets.

Whiting & Davis manufactured the rare compact topped *Dresden* and *Ivorytone* armor mesh purses. *Ivorytone* is an armor mesh purse that has an unusual shiny color scheme. *Dresden* is colored ring mesh. During the twenties, a splendid array of Dresden fine mesh purses were produced. Their name was taken from the German inventor who developed the machine to make this type of fine colored mesh. Especially vibrant in color, they were made with a colored silk screened process giving the purse a surrealistic, watercolor appearance. Whiting & Davis also sold *El-Sah* purses which had an additional metal tag attached on the inside and/or a stamp impressed into the frame. They were made from a variety of patterns, and the *El-Sah* vanity purse is a treasure to find. The compacts on these frames are round and the mesh purses attached are vivid in color. Compacts can be found centered on the frame or off to the side. Linings could be ordered in a bevy of pretty pastel colors. The purse interiors are spacious, with a beveled glass mirror attached to a silk lining with a reinforced silk tab. One in particular called *The Swinging Compact Costume Purse* contains the compact centered in the frame, but instead of sitting rigidly in its place, the compact swings on a hinge. This is a very difficult piece to find, was expensive to purchase originally, and can command a hefty price again today.

The Art Deco style, which became popularized by the *Exposition Internationale des Arts Decoratifs et Industriels Modernes* in Paris in 1925, promoted a new look with geometric shapes and vivid colors that influenced designs of furniture, clothing, jewelry, and vanity purses. Although its heyday was short lived, the style's influence can be seen throughout the subsequent decades. As the economic prosperity of the twenties was eclipsed with the onset of the Great Depression in the thirties, the purses produced by Whiting & Davis changed to accommodate more discerning customers.

In 1938, when Charles A. Whiting's grandson, Charles Whiting Rice, began working for the company the new purses had already changed from colorful enameled mesh to solid gold- or silver-colors. Two years later, Charles A. Whiting died at seventy-six years of age, having been largely responsible for the business's success. In 1960, Charles Rice became president of the company his renowned grandfather helped to make so prosperous. He retired six years later, in 1966, after the company was sold to Certified Pharmaceutical.

Today, The Whiting & Davis Company continues to produce mesh apparel and fashion accessories from the same type of materials, including evening and day wear purses to purses and purse accessories, including coin purses, wallets, checkbook covers, lipstick holders, and eyeglass cases. The fashion department has designed gowns, skirts, and tops for celebrities such as Cher, Elizabeth Taylor, Morgan Fairchild,

and Rita Moreno. Model Christie Brinkley was photographed draped in Whiting & Davis mesh for the cover of *Cosmopolitan* in September 1983. Additionally, they now produce other items for industrial use such as shark proof diving suits, belts, and metal safety gloves for meat cutters. The company moved its factory headquarters to a new location in Massachusetts in 1995 where it reproduced a small selection of enameled mesh purses under the name of The Heritage Collection.

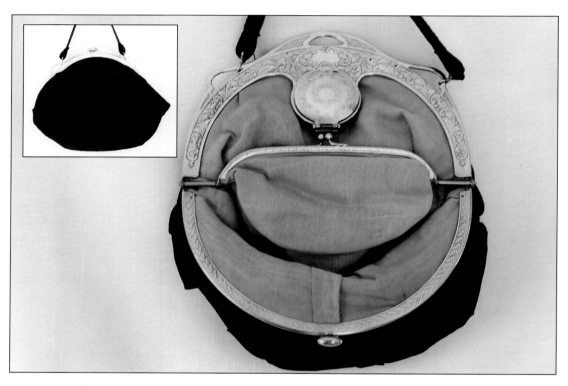

An unmarked vanity purse with a black fabric body. The compact is visible only when the purse is opened. *The Curiosity Shop*. Rare.

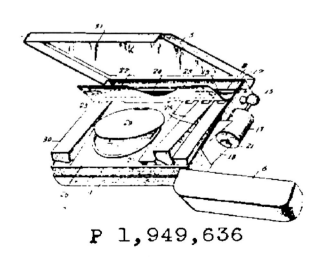

P 1,949,636

Daughters were given vanity purses to match their mother's.

The R & G Company is the most elusive of all the major manufacturers of vanity purses, for nothing is known about them. The R & G purses that exist are of high quality with compact tops of very intricately enameled flowers and foliage in pastel colors on sterling silver. Sturdy wrist straps are made from a tightly woven braid or foxtail mesh. Inside, a round compact section has a mirror and a large receptacle for packed powder. Above the powder on the inside of the lid is a rouge pot behind a generous sized mirror. Below the metal powder container, accessible by lifting the compact section up, is a spacious mesh purse. The metal bands around the outside of the compact are etched in silver flowers. Elaborately enameled or plain armor mesh purses by R & G were available in regular link sizes as well as the finer quality baby flat mesh, half the size of the standard flat mesh links. The purses are embellished with metal chain tassels. Fashionably draped over the arm and adjusted by a mesh wrist strap, it offered little interference to the intricate moves of fancy stepping to the big band sound of jazz that was so popular at this time.

Whiting and Davis vanity purse with textured compact to the front side of frame. Gold plated flat mesh. 4½" x 6½". *The Curiosity Shop.* $500-800.

R&G vanity purse shown with powder patter. 2½" x 7". *The Curiosity Shop.* $500-700.

R&G vanity purse with baby enameled mesh and a sterling enameled lid. 2½" x 7". *From the Collection of Joyce Morgan, Photograph by Harry Barth.* $500-700.

Beautiful vanity purse with compact centered in small frame.
Enameled flat mesh body has a flower basket design. 4" x 7".
Lori Landgrebe Antiques. $450-650.

R&G baby flat enameled mesh with unusual octagon shaped compact top. Shown open to reveal
rouge receptacle, mirror, and powder section. 2½" x 6". *The Curiosity Shop.* $500-700.

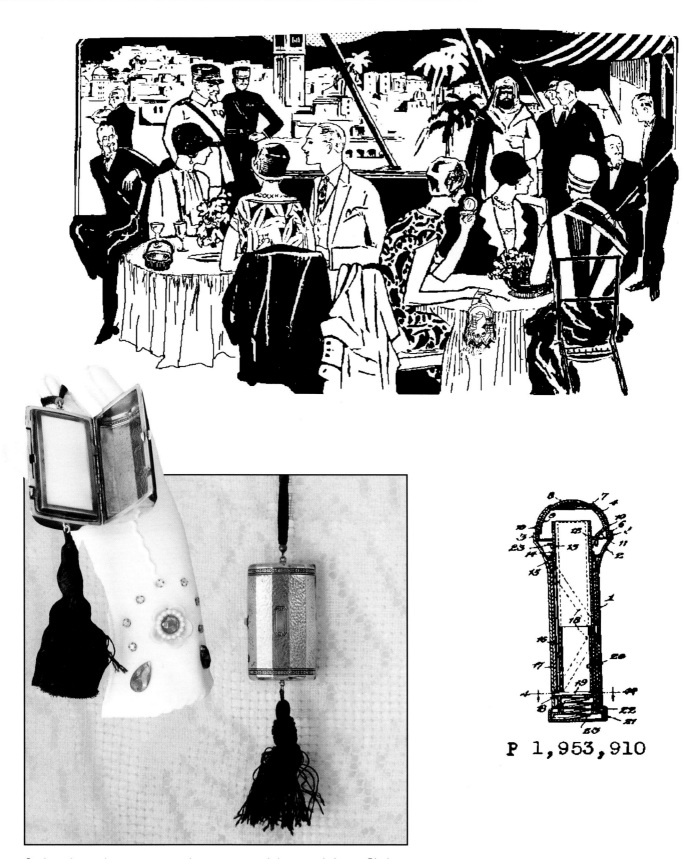

Sterling silver multi-compartmented vanity case with hammered design. Black tassel and carry cord. Also shown open to reveal large compartment and mirror that conceals smaller puff and rouge compartments. 2½" × 3½". *The Curiosity Shop.* $225-275.

P 1,953,910

42156 3½-inch Silver plated Mesh Bag, beautifully enameled frame, fine accordion mesh with lace fringe, fitted with mirror, puff and powder..$25.00

42157 3¾-inch Silver plated Mesh Bag, enameled frame, fine accordion mesh, silk cord handle and fringe, fitted with mirror, puff and powder
........................$20.00

Whiting and Davis enameled mesh vanity purse with a jeweled and mesh shield shaped compact. A tassel hangs from the compact. 4" x 7". *Lori Landgrebe Antiques.* $375-550.

French suede vanity purses are usually black with compact receptacles at the top. Oftentimes, they are cylindrical shaped in various sizes. Inside, they can be found marked, "Paris" or "Made in France" with foil labels on the mirror. The compact portion has compressed powder and a puff. Designs on the fabric vary from rhinestone ornamentation to gold plated, brass buttons, bows, and other designs, fitted with metal tassels.

The Whiting and Davis *Piccadilly* goldtone mesh vanity purse. 2½" x 7". *From the Collection of Sharon Haines*. $150-250.

A black suede French vanity purse shown open to reveal mirror, puff, and powder compartment. Gilt mesh carry strap with gild button decoration. 3" x 5". *The Curiosity Shop*. $150-200.

Shown open.

French black suede vanity purse. The compact is concealed under the lid. Black carry cord, tassel on top, decorated with rhinestone encrusted bows and gilt brass fittings. 3" x 6". *The Curiosity Shop*. $150-200.

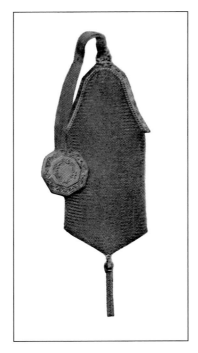

George T. Brodnax, Inc., 1926.

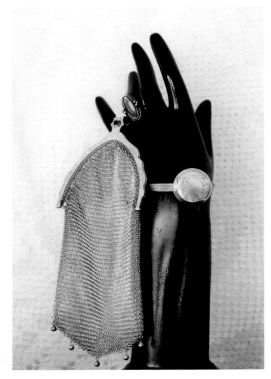

Soldered mesh vanity purse with scalloped frame. It has a foxtail mesh adjustable wrist chain with an attached compact. *The Curiosity Shop*. Rare.

Evans goldtone flat enameled mesh vanity purse with black enameled detail around compact lid. 4" x 4". *The Curiosity Shop*. $125-175.

Evans goldtone flat enameled mesh with finger ring chain. 3" x 4". *The Curiosity Shop*. $125-175.

The Evans Case Company produced mesh vanity purses as well as fabric vanity pouches. Incorporated in 1922 in North Attleboro, Massachusetts, the Evan's vanity purses were manufactured in the 1930s. Their most popular vanity purse has a round, gold plated, or enameled compact top with a flat mesh goldtone body and was distributed in the early part of that decade. One style is oval with enameling on the compact lid. Linings are silk, usually in an ivory color. The Whiting & Davis Company supplied the mesh for The Evans Company, who did not produce nearly the quantity of vanity purses that Whiting & Davis did. The Evans Company also made special mesh vanity purses for sororities and clubs with identifying insignia enameled or stamped onto the frame. Occasionally, the vanity purse would be affixed to a lipstick by a short linked connector called a tango chain. Designs on the lids of these compact tops were relatively simple, for instance, black enameling in simple geometric shapes or applied metal Scottie dogs.

Later in that decade, another type of armor mesh was used in the making of Evans vanity purses. It was called Beadlite. Using this technique, a raised dot in the center of the spider gave the link a three dimensional appearance. When enameled in color, it emulates glass or steel beading used in making other types of vintage purses.

This company also created simple purses with fancy faux jeweled frames that were fitted with compacts, mirrors, and combs. These items were placed in specially made sleeves sewn into silk linings. The Evans insignia could be found sewn into these linings.

The Evans fabric vanity pouch is their most difficult to find today. One example has a guilloché enameled lid, a black satin body embellished with rhinestones, and an off-white taffeta lining. Inside is loose powder, pressed rouge, and a metallic mirror. Carry chains attached to these vanities were made of links or foxtail mesh with some having finger ring attachments. Often, if the rouge is still intact in these Evans' vanity purses, you can see the impressed logo, "Mayfair."

The popular *Piccadilly*. *The Saturday Evening Post*, 1922.

The Whiting and Davis *El-Sah*. 3½" x 7½". *From the Collection of Joyce Morgan, Photograph by Harry Barth*. $350-450.

The Whiting and Davis *Delysia*.
Cosmopolitan, December, 1924.

The Ladies Home Journal, November, 1922.

The *Delysia* in fine soldered mesh. 3" x 6". *From the Collection of Joyce Morgan, Photograph by Harry Barth. Rare.*

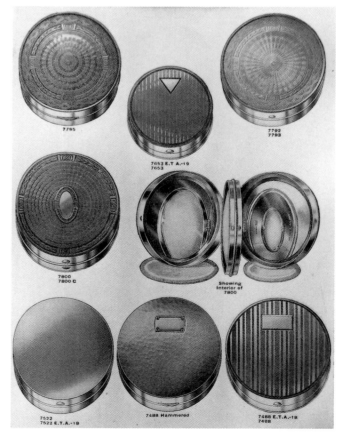

F&B powder compacts. *The Foster Blue Book*, 1925-26.

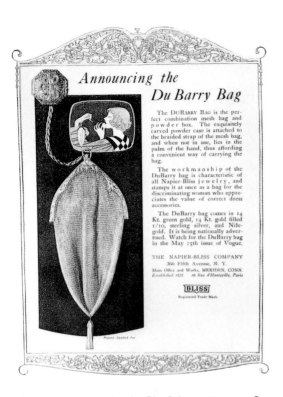

An announcement for the Bliss/Napier *Du Barry* Purse. Attaching the compact to the carry strap instead of the purse frame was an innovative design. *Courtesy of The Napier Company archives*, 1921.

Enameled mesh Whiting and Davis vanity purse with silhouetted figures in a dance pose on the compact lid. 3½" x 7". *From the Collection of Joyce Morgan, Photograph by Harry Barth.* $350-450.

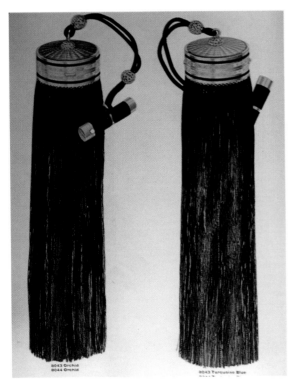

Orchid or turquoise vanities by F&B. A sifter could be purchased for the compact portion for $1.50. *The Foster Blue Book*, 1925.

The Ladies Home Journal, October, 1924.

Whiting and Davis gilded fine mesh vanity purse with etched and engraved lid, extra large compact with tassel pull and wrist chain. Circa: 1920s. 4" x 6". *The Curiosity Shop*. $450-550.

Unusual jeweled topped vanity purse with fabric body. 5" x 7". *The Curiosity Shop*. $175-275.

The *Piccadilly* by Whiting and Davis, soldered mesh vanity purse with blue cabochon thumbclasps, engraved frame with central powder compact and mirror. 5" x 5". *The Curiosity Shop*. $250-300.

Chapter Five

The Compact as Art

The fascinating evolution of the compact is not limited to the actual manufacture of the piece itself, but expands to the cosmetic industry where the art of compact and cosmetic development was achieved by the ingenuity of design and promotion by leaders in the industry. These leaders—like Max Factor, a cosmetic artist—were in as much if not more demand as a famous painter, since their virtues were based on need, not only desire.

Since the time Mary Pickford starred in one-reel features and Gloria Swanson wore a Mack Sennett bathing suit, the motion picture industry has relied on the genius of Max Factor for make-up. Max Factor, a Russian immigrant who set up his first business, a haircutting shop, in 1908, began mixing beauty potions at the age of seven. He portrayed the highest expression of make-up art with his talents. He made his name by not only developing special cosmetics for individual stars according to their coloring and needs, but by personally applying them.

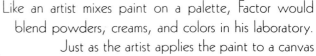

Max Factor, a Russian immigrant, set up his first business, a haircutting shop in 1908. He became a cosmetic artist and since the time Mary Pickford starred in one-reel features and Gloria Swanson wore a Mack Sennett bathing suit, the motion picture industry has relied on the genius of Max Factor for make-up. *The New Art of Society Make-Up*.

Like an artist mixes paint on a palette, Factor would blend powders, creams, and colors in his laboratory. Just as the artist applies the paint to a canvas to create a picture, Factor employed the famous faces of movie stars to display his talent. Professional actors and actresses in England, Germany, France, and America recognized him as the authority on make-up. In 1914 he perfected the first make-up cream for the movies that allowed the actor and actress liberal facial expressions without cracking like the previously used thick greasepaint it was designed to replace.

The impressive Max Factor Building in Hollywood was occupied exclusively by the Max Factor Make-Up Studio and manufacturing laboratories. The studio was a favorite rendezvous of his clientele, the stars of motion pictures.

For years, Factor solved difficult make-up problems for both male and female stars. When Rudolph Valentino needed special make-up for *The Four Horsemen*, Max Factor was there to perfect it. When Douglas Fairbanks wanted a make-up that would not rub off for his role in the *Thief of Bagdad*, Mr. Factor developed it. Rex Ingram had to have underwater make-up for *Mare Nostrum*, so Max Factor was promptly cabled from abroad and the make-up was produced. And when Technicolor pictures presented a new problem of color synchronization, Max Factor again came to the rescue. Countless times, Max Factor's genius has aided a picture or enhanced a star's looks.

There was no doubt that Factor and his make-up became a smashing success in Hollywood. He decided to go public with what he developed as the *Society Make-up line* using the *Color Harmony* principal of assessing an individual's

complexion, hair color, and eye color, then selecting shades of make-up that best complemented the skin type. Factor was then able to offer the opportunity for the general public to share the beauty secrets of Hollywood's Screen Stars. He presented a personalized collection of make-up, harmonized in color to blend perfectly with the complexion and emphasize natural beauty. At last, the public was able to see the wonderful beauty magic in his methods.

When Factor went public with his cosmetic product line he said:

"I believe I have created in cosmetic Color Harmony a life-like naturalness in make-up which every woman will find, as we in Hollywood have proved, to be without equal in accentuating beauty and charm!"

Of course, Max Factor had impeccable credentials after having made up the famous faces of Hollywood's finest including Myrna Loy, Joan Crawford, Lucille Ball, Charlie Chaplin, Fay Wray, Joan Bennett, and Loretta Young. In fact, many of the stars came forward to help him launch his public offering. Since over 95 percent of all make-up used by Hollywood's stars and studios was his, he had little trouble finding celebrity trend setters to voice the praises of his products. So, when he offered his cosmetics to the general public, the same type of make-up that was used in Hollywood, how could he lose?

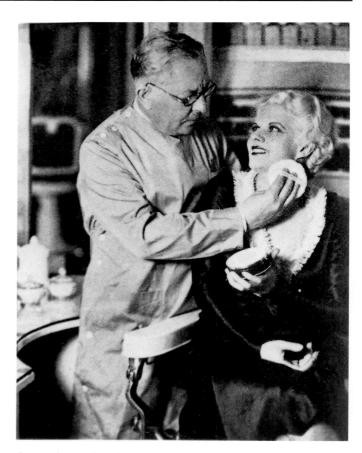

Just as the artist applies paint to a canvas to create a picture, Factor employed the famous faces of movie stars to display his talent. Here, he is shown powdering Jean Harlow's face. *The New Art of Society Make-Up.*

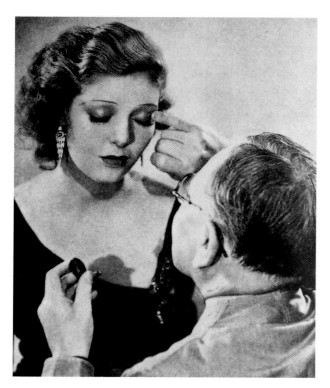

Loretta Young with Factor, who began mixing beauty potions at the age of seven. *The New Art of Society Make-Up.*

Max Factor's award
from the Academy of Motion Picture
Arts and Sciences. *The New Art of Society Make-Up*.

Max Factor discusses his cosmetics line with Joan Crawford. *The New Art of Society Make-Up*.

The stars wrote to the studio regarding his cosmetics. One wrote:

"My Dear Mr. Factor: I am sure that you will be as successful in winning the affection of the public with your new cosmetics as you have for many years those of the stage and screen.
Best of luck,
Laura La Plante."

Joan Bennett was quoted as saying, "The delicate texture and lifelike colorings of your cosmetics make your Society Make-Up incomparable."

Part of his campaign began with a mail order program on a relatively modest basis, by offering a personal complexion analysis with a complete Color Harmony Make-Up Set that sold for $3.95. It included a box containing face powder, rouge, lipstick, eye shadow, eyebrow pencil, make-up blender, cleansing cream, and astringent. The set was sold to those who had responded to an analyzation questionnaire and were then categorized as a specific color type. He offered 10,000 of the original Color Harmony Boxes.

Max Factor applying make-up on Joan Crawford. *Make-up Hints by Max Factor.*

BARBARA STANWYCK
RKO-Radio

POWDER

IN HOLLYWOOD we consider the shade of powder extremely important because we know that the correct color harmony tone can definitely enliven the beauty of the skin.

This is the reason why *Max Factor Hollywood* created original color harmony shades of powder to harmonize with each and every complexion. Each shade is a creation of genius...the color is delicate, subtle, yet it has the warmth and life of compelling beauty.

You will be thrilled with the difference the very first time you make up. Your color harmony shade will impart flattering beauty to your complexion. Soft and fine in texture, *Max Factor Hollywood* Face Powder will create a clinging satin-smooth make-up that hours later will still be lovely.

HOW TO APPLY IT

1.

START powdering at the lower part of the cheeks. Gently pat and blend powder toward center of face. Powder the nose last; otherwise the nose will be over-powdered, making it appear conspicuous.

2.

NOW with the powder puff, press powder lightly into the tiny lines around the eyes, nose, mouth and chin. This assures a completely powdered surface.

3.

WITH the *Max Factor Hollywood* Face Powder Brush, lightly brush away surplus powder, clearing all lines at the eyes, nose, mouth and chin, giving your make-up a velvety, even finish.

ANNE SHIRLEY
RKO-Radio

Make-up Hints by Max Factor.

Jewel-like Compacts

The richness of black and gold . . . the smart simplicity of modern art . . . give a jewel-like elegance to these compacts created by Max Factor that is distinctive and refined.

DOUBLE VANITY
Loose-powder style, complete with Max Factor's Rouge, with a compartment for your color harmony shade in powder.

Blondeen, Raspberry $1.50

EYELASH MAKE-UP
A new-type mascara that will not burn or smart; will not run or smear; will not make eyelashes brittle or break off.

Black, Brown, Blue $1.00

SUPER-INDELIBLE LIPSTICK
The perfect lipstick! Super-Indelible! Colors alive with beauty. Creamy! Soothing and protecting. Satin-smooth!

Flame, Vermillion, Carmine, Crimson $1

PURSE-SIZE EYEBROW PENCIL
A new size in Max Factor's Dermatograph Eyebrow Pencil. Soft and rich in color: non-greasy.

Black or Brown 50

Page Forty-six

Make-up Hints by Max Factor.

Advertisement for Max Factor's doll face mirror which includes two "Hi-Society Lipsticks" in the handle of the mirror.

Special INTRODUCTORY OFFER

Your Own Color Harmony
in MAX FACTOR'S
Society MAKE-UP

TO introduce to the women of America the amazing beauty power of individual Color Harmony Make-Up in its completeness, Max Factor has produced a special make-up box, to sell at the remarkably low price of $3.95.

Attractively packed in New Modern Art Design Box
$3.95

THIS special make-up box contains all the nine essentials of Color Harmony Make-Up which would be $6.50 regularly. It is not a week-end box, sample box or box of small sizes. All cosmetics are in full size packages, excepting three, thus permitting the special introductory price of $3.95.

Think of it! Your complete color harmony in Society Make-Up . . . nine "Cosmetics of the Stars," in modern art box, for $3.95.

This Special
MODERN ART BOX
Contains

(1) **Face Powder**	(full size)
(2) **Rouge**	(full size)
(3) **Lipstick or Pomade**	(full size)
(4) **Eye Shadow**	(full size)
(5) **Masque**	(full size)
(6) **Eyebrow Pencil**	(full size)
(7) **Liquid Whitener**	(half size)
(8) **Cleansing Cream**	(half size)
(9) **Powder Foundation or Honeysuckle Cream**	(half size)

[*ONLY 10,000 Boxes have been produced. All orders will be filled in rotation as they are received. Immediate delivery cannot be promised after this initial quantity has been exhausted. MAIL YOUR ORDER IN AT ONCE.*]

GUARANTEE
We guarantee the quality of Max Factor's Society Make-Up to be the finest obtainable regardless of price.
If for any reason you are not completely satisfied with any merchandise purchased, you may return it and your money will be refunded.
MAX FACTOR STUDIOS, *Hollywood*

Note: *Max Factor's Society Make-Up, the Cosmetic Sensation of the age, is being distributed as fast as our corps of cosmeticians can train and appoint authorized Max Factor Make-Up dealers. Any druggist or cosmetic counter will gladly order this special Make-Up Box for you from Hollywood, packed with your own individual color harmony make-up, or if you prefer, send your order to Max Factor Studios.*

ORDER BLANK. Send thru your dealer or Mail direct to Max Factor Studios, Hollywood.

MAX FACTOR'S MAKE-UP STUDIO, Hollywood, Calif.

I enclose $3.95 (check, bills, or P. O. money order), for which please send me the complete Color Harmony Make-Up Set, packed in New Modern Art Design Box. I have written the color wanted in each cosmetic in the chart at the left, according to my complexion analysis.

NAME.

ADDRESS.

CITY. STATE.

Your Druggist's Name.

(NOTE: If you wish to order additional items also, see the "Complete Price List and Order Blank" enclosed.)

Max Factor's make-up studio and manufacturing laboratories, Hollywood, California. The studio was a favorite rendezvous of his clientele, the stars of motion pictures. Like an artist mixes paint on a palette, Factor would blend powders, creams, and colors in his laboratory. Both are now home to the Max Factor Museum.

In his studio, Max Factor continued to produce marvels of make-up, not only for the stars of stage and screen, but for everyone who sent in the color information chart. And, it was only natural that his revolutionary discoveries in cosmetic color coordination, in addition to purity and fineness, earned popularity and widespread endorsement, becoming a successful introduction that became the beginning of a long-term, flourishing campaign which reached the general public. Soon, drug stores, using the world's first make-up chart developed by Factor, were able to help the customer determine which products would work best with her natural coloring. Cleverly, with the use of this "Color Harmony" principal, Factor was able to sell three different products bearing his label; i.e., face powder, rouge, and lipstick, to each customer instead of the usual single sale item.

In letters written to Max Factor's studio in 1941, the make-up secrets of Lana Turner, Betty Grable, and Rita Hayworth were requested. He went on to invent waterproof mascara, and it was not long before Factor's cosmetics were available everywhere.

The world famous Hollywood Make-up Salon is now a public beauty museum filled with artifacts and movie memorabilia, spanning over decades of cosmetic innovation. Displays include: the strange looking beauty calibrator, resembling a catcher's mask, loaded with thumb screws and flexible metal bands that was invented to measure the faces of screen stars; hundreds of autographed photos of the celebrities whose beauty he enhanced; vintage advertisements; and the Kissing Machine. Factor died at age 91 at his West Los Angeles home in 1996.

Salvador Felipe Jacinto Dali was a Spanish painter born May 11, 1904. Dali took an early interest in painting and the figurative arts as well as all types of creative expression and activity. He took private lessons in painting at an early age from a professor at the Academy of Art. His first paintings clearly show the influences of Spanish artists.

Dali was an unusual and eccentric character who spent a short time in prison in 1924, apparently for political reasons, and was expelled from the Academy of Art in 1926. He had the opportunity to meet Picasso in Paris, but they were so different from each other that they were unable to become friends.

Salvador Dali.

Still, Dali, with his unconventional style became a famous artist who displayed his work at great surrealist exhibitions in Paris and at the New York World's Fair in 1939, before he went on to create one of the most exciting compacts ever made.

The "Bird-In-Hand" compact is a three dimensional piece in the shape of a bird, less than the size of an open hand, designed by Salvador Dali in conjunction with the famous compact manufacturer, Elgin American. Dali's signature is in black on the bird's head which pulls out to reveal a lipstick. When opened, The Elgin American logo is visible on the hinged powder compartment. The tail lifts open for use as a pillbox. The bird's wings do not part, but rather lift open. The goldtone and sterling cases are less common than the silvered case with goldtone feather highlights.

This unusual compact, expensive and available in exclusive shops, was advertised as:

"The exultant expression of an artist's dream...lofty spirit of fashion, released from all earthbound tradition. Available to the favored few...designed for the hands of those who love loveliness...those who are ever first to forsake the commonplace. From such threads of imagination are all Elgin American creations spun...brought into immortal being expressly for those whom fashion follows. A masterpiece by Elgin American, compact, lipstick, pillbox ...all in one! Elgin American interprets a Dali flight of fancy."

Vogue, 1951.

A pair of Salvador Dali designed "Bird-In-Hand" compacts by Elgin American. Left: silvertone finish with gold highlighted feathers, right: goldtone. 4½" x 2". *The Curiosity Shop*. Left, rare; right, very rare.

Elgin American "Bird-In-Hand" goldtone vanity case designed by Salvador Dali. Dali's signature is in black on the bird's head which pulls out and reveals a lipstick. When opened as shown here, The Elgin American logo is visible on the hinged powder compartment. The tail lifts open for use as a pillbox. 4½" x 2". *The Curiosity Shop*.

The Original by Robert compact chair was available as part of a dresser set which included a tray, picture frame, lipstick container, and various other pieces. The artists that founded the company in 1949, Robert Levy, David Jaffe, and Irking Landsman, joined later by Larry Joseph, was formerly known as Fashioncraft. In 1960, the name of the company was changed to Robert Originals, Inc.

The company was well known for dramatic costume jewelry pieces that carried the name of "Robert," as well as "Original by Robert." Often, these brooches, necklaces, and bracelets had intricate prong set rhinestones combined with tiny faux pearls and metal goldtone ornamentation, similar to the designs plainly visible on the compact chairs.

The vanity chairs, quite an ingenious design, have round seats that lift up to reveal powder puff and sifter, along with a small well to store loose powder. The chairs stand on sturdy metal legs, and in some cases, have traces of enameling. Ornamentation on the chairs can also include enameled flowers in pink and white with rhinestone centers and accents. The oval-like shield that carries the "Original by Robert" signature is in the shape of an artist's palette and is on the bottom portion located at the back of the chair. Green felt pads on the underside of the seat conceal the compact case manufacturer called "Majestic." The company changed names to Ellen Designs, Inc. in 1984.

"Original by Robert" signed compact chairs. The seats lift up to reveal puff, sifter, and powder cavity. To the left: jewel encrusted seat and chair back with pink enameled flowers, the legs of the chair are enameled white. To the right: faux jewels and pearls on the seat's back and leg fronts. Also stamped "Majestic." Center: lipstick cases signed "Original by Robert." 2½" x 5". *Author's Collection*. Rare.

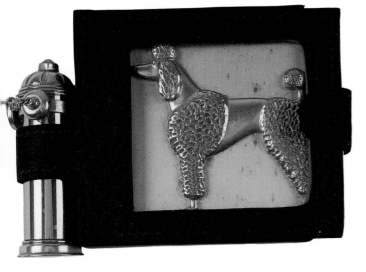

Signed "Original by Robert" on the material, this amusing compact has an applied goldtone poodle on its lid, the interior puff also has Robert logo. The lipstick is in the shape of a fire hydrant. 3" x 3½". *From the Collection of Joan Orlen, Photograph by Steven Freeman Photography*. Rare.

Majestic Metal Specialties, Inc. manufactured the unusual vanity chair signed "Original by Robert." *The American Perfumer*, 1934.

French 1920s doll holding compact and puff. *Lori Landgrebe Antiques*. No value available.

The dangerous nature of celluloid was known as early as 1910 when drying furnaces were not allowed to exceed 113 degrees for fear of explosion. At left: early interior factory photographs show workers drawing tubes of celluloid. Bottom right: cutting out celluloid rods. Top right: rolling sheets of celluloid. *Scientific American*.

Strips of celluloid thick enough to be used in compact making had to remain in drying chambers for up to six months. Top: bending celluloid hairpins. Right: blowing celluloid dolls. *Scientific American*, 1910.

Compacts that have been molded or carved from celluloid have a charm unlike their counterparts made of metal or other materials. As a result of the dangerous nature of celluloid, it is no longer manufactured, and these compacts are a true representation of the unwitting time they emerged from. While many vanity cases are collectible and no longer made for various reasons, those made of celluloid have a collectible edge because of the material they are derived from. They are easier to date since celluloid was no longer manufactured after 1934 when it was banned from the market by federal law.

Prior to 1850, chemists began the search for substances to imitate horn, tortoise shell, bone, and ivory for use in a variety of items including hair combs, dentures, photographic film, tooth brushes, fountain pens, piano keys, purses, compacts, dolls, and jewelry. Dr. Pierson of New Orleans discovered celluloid, which is a complex substance consisting chiefly of nitrocellulose and camphor in 1848. Celluloid was the trade name given to the material by its inventor,

John Wesley Hyatt, who in 1869 began using it for industry. The manufacture of celluloid was begun by the Hyatt brothers in Newark, New Jersey, in 1867. Other large celluloid factories were subsequently established in America, France, England, and Germany.

Celluloid was widely used from 1890 to 1917 when it was made from a very pure form of cellulose, usually obtained from raw or spun cotton or filter paper. The cellulose was converted into nitrocellulose by varying methods, depending on the manufacturer. Among the processes were the following: cotton or paper was chopped or cut into strips, then immersed in nitric acid for a period ranging from fifteen minutes to two hours, according to the character of the fibers and the temperature of the bath. The cotton or paper was then converted into nitrocellulose. It was taken out, wrung, and pressed to remove most of the adhering liquid, which may or may not have been returned to the nitrating bath. In either case, the bath was restored to its original strength by the addition of concentrated nitric acid.

Black celluloid vanity case with faux jewels imbedded in design. Tassels on either side of compact with celluloid fittings on carry cord. 4½" x 6". *The Curiosity Shop*. $350-450.

Shown open to reveal mirror, pocket, powder ring, and lipstick holder.

The nitrocellulose was washed in water and ground in a paper mill, whereby a rotary movement was pressed on the mass as it was forced between a plate and two cylinders which rotated at a speed of 160 revolutions per minute. Next, nitrocellulose made a journey to the bleachery for treatment. Then, celluloid was made by dissolving nitrocellulose in an alcoholic solution of camphor. It was pressed, rolled, cut, and processed before drying.

Even as early as 1910, according to the trade magazine *The Scientific American*, the danger of using celluloid was known. Here, they indicated that celluloid was dried in chambers where the temperature was never allowed to exceed 113 degrees because of the dangerous possibility of explosion. Strips thick enough to make compacts had to stay in the drying chamber for about six months. The celluloid bands were then shaped, cut out, molded, curved, varnished, and decorated. Blowing was performed on celluloid tubes as they were drawn from the press. A tube of suitable dimension was placed in a heated mold composed of two or more segments, and when soft, was inflated by a blast of high pressure steam, forcing the celluloid into contact with every part of the mold that was cooled before opening. In this way, whisk broom covers and similar cup-shaped objects, as well as dolls, animal figures, compacts, and toys were made. Parts of celluloid boxes and other built-up objects were sometimes joined by means of acetone, acetic acid, or other solvents of celluloid.

A mirror is inside the lid of this unique egg-shaped Bakelite vanity purse. 2½" x 4". *From the Collection of Joyce Morgan, Photograph by Harry Barth*. Rare.

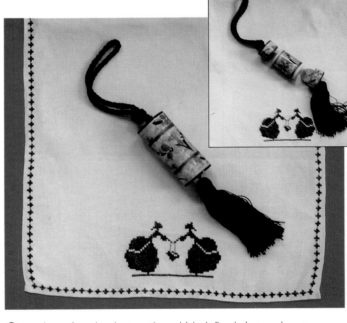

Oriental motif, early plastic, gilt and black floral designed vanity case with rhinestone embedded bolster shape. Circa: 1920s. The vanity case unscrews at the top and bottom to reveal a mirror, puff, powder, and rouge cavity with a receptacle for small items. 1½" dia. x 3½". *The Curiosity Shop*. $350-500.

Bolster shaped early plastic vanities. The red is shown open with lipstick in tassel revealed. Circa: 1920s. 1½" dia. x 3½". *The Curiosity Shop*. $350-500.

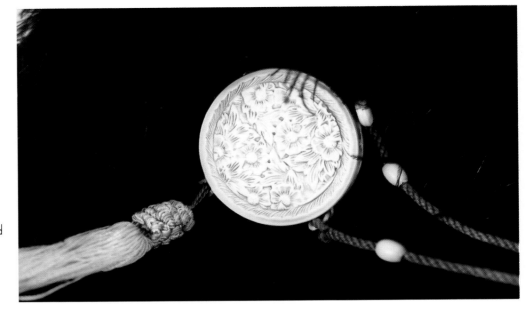

Tasseled ivory colored celluloid pressed vanity in a floral design containing a powder receptacle and mirror. Carry cord has celluloid fittings. 3" dia. *The Curiosity Shop*. $225-325.

Inexpensive boxes were varnished with a solution of celluloid in acetic acid, which saved polishing with pumice stone. For decorating the surface, aniline colors dissolved in alcohol were employed.

Many celluloid compacts were shaped by hand, much like wood, horn and ivory which celluloid was invented to replace. This was accomplished by a worker using a chisel, drawing knife, rasp, etc. Flat compacts with curved contours were cut out with band saws. A number of sheets to be used for compacts were cut at once and oiled paper was interposed between the sheets of celluloid to prevent the sawdust from clogging the saw. To provide curves in the compact, the worker took advantage of the plasticity which celluloid acquires when it is gently heated.

Celluloid hair pins were pointed on an emery wheel. Shaping was done on a lathe. Cutting was accomplished preferably by machine, with punches, and circular and band saws, employing cutting wheels with straight and fluted edges. Thin, celluloid hair pins were immersed in hot water, bent by hand on a metal form, and quickly hardened by being plunged into cold water. All operations had to be performed with skill and care, as celluloid became white and opaque when heated too quickly or strongly.

Early plastic compact with red and black carving. Opens to reveal puff, receptacle for powder, and mirror. Plastic loops around the compact keep the carry cord in place. 4" dia. *The Curiosity Shop.* $175-325.

Celluloid objects of a variety of forms, including compacts, were produced by molding, in which the softening influence of heat was again utilized. For example, a compact, approximately shaped by other methods, was inserted between two segments of a bronze compact mold which were in contact with the heated plates of a steam press. When the celluloid had become sufficiently plastic, the plates were forced together, and the celluloid assumed the exact form of the compact mold, which it retained after cooling. Leaves, flower petals, small thin objects, and similar compact ornamentation made of celluloid were shaped by stamping with dies.

Celluloid was plentiful, inexpensive, and easy to work into a variety of shapes. A variety of faux jewels and pearls could easily be imbedded into celluloid compacts for decoration before they hardened completely. Although the creation of celluloid compacts was quite an extensive one, the material was much more plentiful than the previously used ivory, bone, horn, and tortoise shell. During this time, manual labor was not expensive, and the material itself was not costly. It was only until it was banned by federal law that industry ceased the manufacture of celluloid.

Vintage Compacts & Beauty Accessories

A rare, early plastic bolster shaped compact purse. 2½" x 5". *From the Collection of Joyce Morgan, Photograph by Harry Barth*. Rare.

Black celluloid, 1920s, French floral rhinestone and faux pearl encrusted, black carry cord and silk tassel. The tassel is capped with a celluloid fitting and conceals a lipstick. This vanity had to be made with skill and care, as celluloid became white and opaque when heated too quickly or strongly. Shown open, the compact reveals mirror, puff, powder and rouge separated by a perfume or lipstick receptacle. 3" x 4". *From the Collection of Paula Higgins*. $350-450.

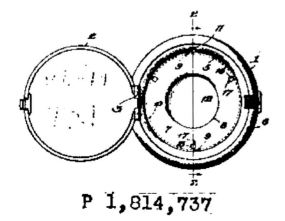

P 1,814,737

Ivory colored celluloid pressed vanity containing a mirror. 3" dia. *The Curiosity Shop*. $175-275.

5260—A Powder Box and Puff. Very smart. Made of transparent celluloid with rose decorations. A fine velour puff in pink to harmonize with box. Diameter, 4½ inches..................................... 1.00

The Pohlson Galleries Gift Book.

Left: French celluloid dual opening compact with lipstick concealed in tassel and gold painting and amber rhinestones embedded into the cover. 2" x 4". Right: Unusual lightly carved and rhinestone embedded compact with lipstick in tassel. 3" x 5". *The Curiosity Shop.* Left, $275-375; right, $250-350.

Celluloid powder box and puff with hand painted lid pictured shown with a hand painted wallet. These powder boxes sold in novelty catalogs for approximately one dollar. 4½" dia. *The Curiosity Shop.* $25-35.

Early plastic compact with crosshatching and teal blue rhinestones embedded into cover. Black carry cord and tassel. 2" x 4". *Lori Landgrebe Antiques.* $150-200.

American Colt purse make-up kit with black and white tubular container. Shown with original box. Designed with several sections for favorite powders, rouges, creams, etc, to be filled after purchase. Circa: 1930s. 1" x 3½". *The Curiosity Shop.* $40-60.

Deeply carved Bakelite vanity with original silk tassel, clock face embedded into the compact lid. 2" x 4". *Author's Collection.* Very rare.

Shown open, the mirrored top of the compact portion is visible and the hinged storage compartment opens with a pull of the tassel.

The American Perfumer, 1931.

Bolster shaped compacts from the 1920s were made of early plastic, probably Bakelite, and came with a carry cord and fringed tassel. The tassel almost always concealed a lipstick tube, thereby saving space in these small compacts for rouge and powder. Mirrors were located on the inside, along with cavities for rouge, puff, and powder, as well as a receptacle for trinkets. Access to these areas could be gained by unscrewing either of the threaded portions of the plastic. Available in many designs and colors, these vanities are small and hang nicely on the wrist.

The material called Bakelite, the trademark name of phenolic synthetic resin, was discovered in 1909 by Leo Hendrik Baekelund (1863-1944), a Belgian American Chemist, in his private laboratory in Yonkers, New York. It was formed by the combination of phenol and formaldehyde often compounded with reinforcing fillers such as wood fibers or cotton linters. Under the influence of heat, it became a hard, insoluble mass which is incombustible. In its pure form, it is colorless or light golden resembling celluloid in appearance, yet much harder and heavier.

The General Bakelite Company was organized in 1910. In 1922, the company merged with two others to form The Bakelite Corporation. In just a short time after this, Bakelite flooded the marketplace. It was made into costume jewelry, poker chips, bottle caps, electric switches, cutlery handles, vanity purses, and compacts. Colorful bangles, fruit shaped necklaces, and multi-colored geometric jewelry could be purchased at the five and dime stores. The variety of colors soon became astounding and clever accessorizing was affordable! Soon, many other firms marketed phenolic resin under other trade names.

Lucite and Plexiglas are the trade names for polymethyl methacrylate (PMMA), also called acrylic. PMMA is a substance that prevents crystallization and has a high resistance to ultraviolet radiation and the outdoor elements. It is hard and strong with the potential for unlimited coloring possibilities, although it can be brittle. Other than compacts, Lucite has been used for lighting fixtures, outdoor signs, and automobile taillights. Compacts made from Lucite are often found to be translucent. Shortly after came acetate which was made to simulate tortoiseshell, a natural substance used like a plastic in earlier years.

The *Trio-ette by Platé* was made of molded Tenite, an early form of plastic. It was called a triple compact because one side consisted of powder, puff, and sifter. The other side had rouge and a puff, while the matching lipstick was cleverly concealed in the handle. The raised rose design on the lid of the compact was inspired by a quaint Victorian rose cameo hand mirror. Distributed by the House of Platé in Detroit, Michigan, and available in most stores, it could be obtained in ebony, ivory, green, tortoise, pink, and blue. Compatible refills were also available.

The American Perfumer, 1933.

Belle Ayre Lucite flapjack with translucent faceted case, puff with logo, mirror. 5" dia. *The Curiosity Shop*. $80-100.

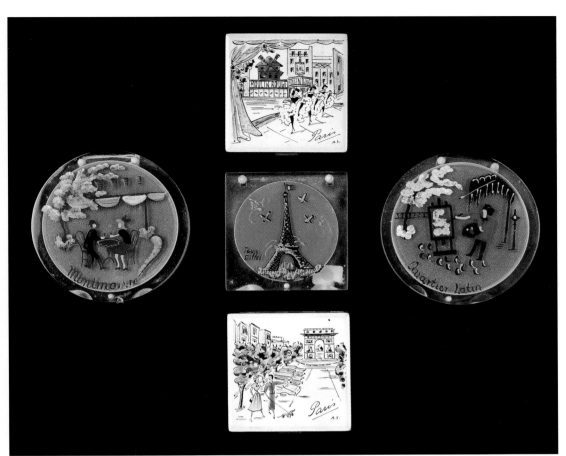

Three colorful and clever center compacts of Lucite; the center left depicts the famous area where paintings are made in France, center is the Eiffel Tower, and at the right is the Latin Quarter with a picture of an artist painting. $175-275 each. The top and bottom compacts are hand colored by the same artist. The top says, "Moulin rouge, Paris." $125-150 each. All of these compacts are French souvenirs and hand painted, Bell DeLuxe is the manufacturer. The square compacts have beveled mirrors and receptacles for loose powder, measuring 3" x 3". Rounds are 4" dia. *From the Collection of Joan Orlen, Photograph by Steven Freeman Photography.*

The *Trio-ette* by Platé in mint green, shown open to reveal puff, powder, mirror section, and lipstick in handle. 3" x 4½". *The Curiosity Shop*. $125-250.

The *Trio-ette* triple compact made of molded Tenite. One side consists of powder sifter and puff, the other, rouge with lipstick in the handle. Originally sold for approximately five dollars, 1940s.

Another artistic form of creating compacts was with hand stitched needlework and petitpoint designs. It became fashionable to learn and practice various forms of needlework in the nineteenth century. Considered a common pastime, it was perfect for the sewing rooms that many large Victorian houses had come equipped with, thus a satisfying diversion for those who had little other entertainment.

To cover the open space between the warp and weft threads using a needle laden with thread, usually silk, of stitches taken across from one opening in the canvas to the next in a diagonal direction is called *needlepoint*. Extremely fine work is accomplished when the stitch is half the size of the completed needlepoint stitch. The procedure is then called *petitpoint*. A small area of petitpoint, enough to cover a modestly sized compact of about forty stitches to the square inch, could take as long as four hundred hours to chart and stitch. A micro-stitch (approximately sixty stitches to the square inch) would take much longer. When the stitch is large, nearing twice the area of the needlepoint stitch, the method becomes known as *gross point*.

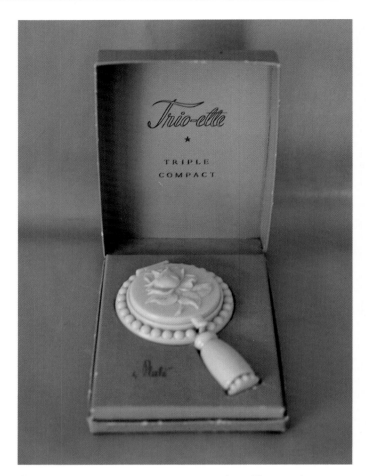

The ivory colored *Trio-ette* in presentation box. The raised rose design on the lid of the compact was inspired by a quaint Victorian rose cameo hand mirror. Distributed by the House of Platé in Detroit, Michigan, and available in most stores, it could be obtained in ebony, ivory, green, tortoise, pink, and blue. Compatible refills were also available. 3" x 4½". *The Curiosity Shop*. $125-200.

A small area of petitpoint, enough to cover a modestly sized compact with about forty stitches to the square inch, could take as long as four hundred hours to chart and stitch.

Lovely petitpoint figural. 3" x 4½". *Lori Landgrebe Antiques*. $150-250.

A fine petitpoint figural compact depicting a Victorian musical scene, containing as many as forty stitches per square inch. 4" x 4". *Author's Collection*. $175-275.

Tapestry stitch is used in embroidery and in *Berlin* work. This stitch is raised from the canvas by virtue of padding the braid. The padding improves the stitch tremendously, otherwise it lies flat as a result of not being crossed. It is worked over two horizontal threads. Compact lids made of tapestry were machine or hand woven.

In the early twentieth century, petitpoint and needlework compacts were made as a hobby, eventually to be used for personal enjoyment. Creating the needlework design for compacts was a pleasant undertaking since they were small, and the task was not overwhelming when compared to the amount of stitching required to make a purse or pillow. Soon, needlework and petitpoint stitching became a cottage industry and the fruits of the labor were sold to manufacturers. Often, this was accomplished in European countries. Once the needlework was completed, the manufacturer fitted the fancy needlework with compact cases, which were then exported for sale.

The creation of many compacts and vanity cases was a form of artwork in itself, since it had to be meticulously handled, as in the case of early plastics, or tenderly stitched in cases where petitpoint and needlework were utilized. Either way, the work was accomplished by hand in most cases, and was time consuming. But in both instances, the procedures in which they were created are virtually a thing of the past.

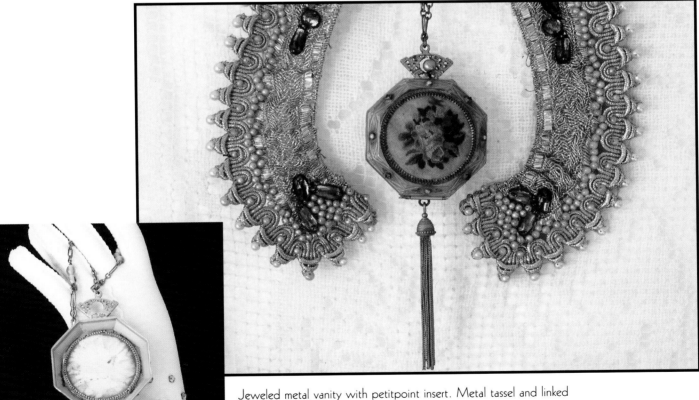

Jeweled metal vanity with petitpoint insert. Metal tassel and linked wrist chain. 4" dia. *The Curiosity Shop.* $250-350.

Needleworked floral on netted gauze. Detailed embossing
around the middle of the compact. 2½" dia.
The Curiosity Shop. $75-100.

Petitpoint figural/floral square compact. 4" x 4".
The Curiosity Shop. $85-125.

Chapter Six
Manufacturers

In the 1920s, the female population was steadily buying compacts, talc, and powder boxes, and the demand continued to increase. By 1927, women so busily powdered their noses that cosmetic powder filling had to be accomplished by a quick machine. This automatic powder filling machine was made by a company called Stokes and stocked twenty compacts per minute. Due to its continuing demand, in 1933, an advanced, redesigned version filled more than twice that amount. This relatively new invention was obviously a popular choice for manufacturers who were better able to accommodate the ever-increasing demand.

The Theodore W. Foster & Brothers Company in Providence, Rhode Island, offered unusual pear shaped Foster vanities with mesh carry chain and tassels that sold wholesale for seventy-two to ninety dollars in the mid-Twenties. They are engine turned and consist of an engraved border on the front and back. The interior reveals a large mirror, memorandum tablet and a small space for necessities. On the other side are compartments for a powder puff and change. Often, these special pieces came with a designated shield for a monogram.

Karess round compact with a silvertone lid, enameled with the profile of a woman. The interior has a double mirror, two puffs, and receptacles for powder and rouge. 1¾" dia. *From the Collection of Carol Schwartz, Photograph by Walter Kitik.* $80-150.

Another exceptional item of workmanship by this manufacturer is the bolster shaped sterling silver vanity with an enameled, engine turned cover in various colors. Compartments for powder, rouge, and puffs are found under the lid, along with a mirror and a memo tablet. The bolster shaped body of the purse was often used for carrying small items, but was originally advertised as a cologne vial holder or cigarette case. This rigid metal compartment is concealed by a long silk fringe in a color that corresponds with the enameling on the lid. Lipsticks were usually enameled black and attached on the end of a black silk adjustable wrist cord decorated with gilt filigree ball slides. Refills for lipsticks, powders, and rouge, along with sifters, allowed the customer to use her favorite choice of loose powder.

In 1933, compacts were introduced to potential buyers much like they are in finer establishments today. Stores like Bloomingdales had female employees, called demonstrators, who would have access to samples of a particular product such as powder compacts, perfumes, or other toiletry items. These salespeople, situated behind a cosmetic counter, wore a name badge along with the name of the cosmetic line which they represented. Their job was based on direct customer contact by illustrating the use of the product on interested, prospective customers with the obvious goal of making a sale. Some stores adopted the technique of presenting counter cards for customer viewing. These plaques simply provided the manufacturer's name which included the demonstrator's name and were prominently displayed on the countertop. Many fine collectible compacts found today were once purchased from such a demonstrator in these stores.

Karess
Face Powder

Packaged especially
for the boudoir $2⁰⁰

*Endorsed by
Women of
Discrimination
and Refinement
Everywhere!*

WOODWORTH
Creators of Exclusive Face Powders since 1854
NEW YORK · PARIS

The New Yorker, 1928.

1933
No. 15-C
Powder Filler
(*up to 45 per minute*)

Automatic powder filler machine, servicing up to 45 compacts or powder boxes per minute. *American Perfumer*, 1933.

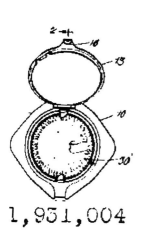

1,931,004

The manufacturing plant of Theodore W. Foster & Brother Company in Providence, Rhode Island. *The Foster Blue Book*, 1925-26.

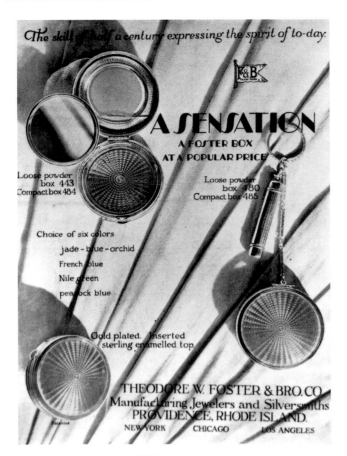

The Jewelers' Circular, 1930.

The Foster Blue Book, 1925-26.

F&B enameled sterling double powder box with lipstick
and finger ring. *The Jewelers' Circular* 1930.

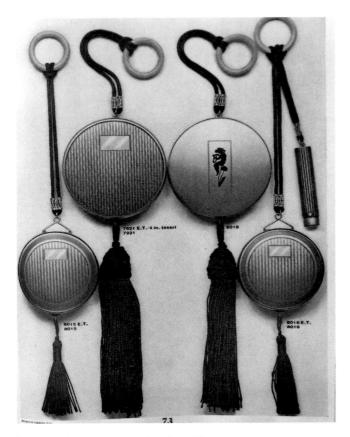

F&B powder compacts with celluloid finger rings. *The Foster Blue Book*, 1925-26.

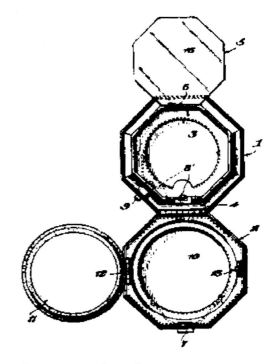

#1,875,127. Patent for a vanity case to Theodore W. Foster & Brother Co., Providence, Rhode Island.

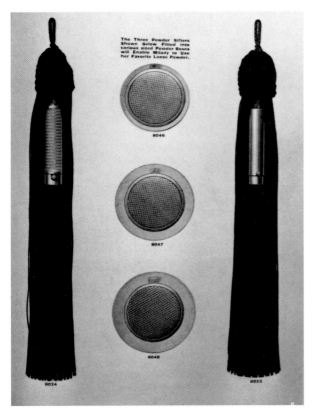

F&B powder sifter and lipstick tassel refills. *The Foster Blue Book*, 1925-26.

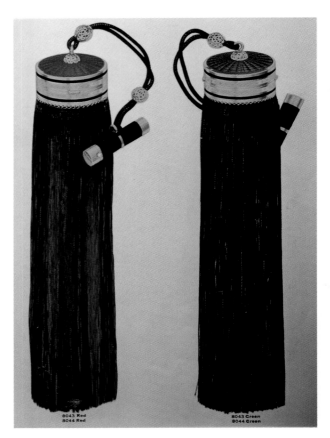

These F&B vanities were made of sterling silver and sold between fifty and sixty dollars in red or green, in either the *Romantic* or *Oriental* designs. *The Foster Blue Book*, 1925.

Rowell powder and rouge boxes made an attractive display on cosmetic counters and in showcases. *The American Perfumer*, 1935.

Successful manufacturers were exceptionally busy as each holiday season drew near. It was a time to take a critical look at their products and make necessary changes according to the advice of their hired experts. Compact cases, labels, and boxes were items that were often subcontracted by the powder manufacturer. Making sure that packaging appealed to the intended consumer was of critical importance. Manufacturers referred to labels as "the personality of the package," and they knew that it had to impart beauty, dignity, and eye appeal.

Compact and powder making companies hired outside professionals used only to design and manufacture their cases, boxes, and packaging. Competition for these contracts was stiff. Catchy labels were made of metal, paper, or foil. Stanley Manufacturing of Dayton, Ohio, specialized in embossed metal and foil labels. Some of Stanley's clients included Charles of the Ritz, Dorothy Perkins, and Tre-jur. Bridgeport Metal Goods Manufacturing Company and other companies produced vanity and rouge cases, lipstick holders, and metal novelties made to the specifications of the customer. Color, texture, and other concerns were seriously considered so that the product would stand out from the hundreds of others available. F.N. Burt Company, Ltd. of Buffalo, New York, and Toronto, Canada, was a leading manufacturer of specialty boxes. Shiny, colorful boxes of expensive quality and vast appeal were designed and created by Burt. Rowell paper rouge and powder boxes gave a touch of unmistakable quality which made an attractive display on cosmetic counters and in showcases.

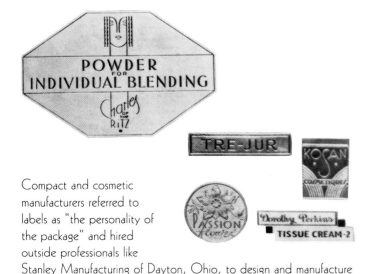

Compact and cosmetic manufacturers referred to labels as "the personality of the package" and hired outside professionals like Stanley Manufacturing of Dayton, Ohio, to design and manufacture them. *The American Perfumer*, 1935.

The American Perfumer, 1932.

Sagamor combined mechanical ingenuity with fine craftsmanship while manufacturing compact cases, loose powder sifters, lipstick containers, and rouge and mascara cases. The Sagamor Captive loose powder vanity was part of a striking window display campaign in New York. The vanity was designed on an entirely new principle patented by Sagamor in the early 1930s. It held a generous supply of powder and an exceptionally heavy puff. Companies like these were retained strictly to create an alluring package with the consumer's enchantment in mind. Some can be found today with the company's name imprinted on their packages, and those found in their original boxes increase their value greatly.

Bridgeport Metal Goods Manufacturing Company produced vanity and rouge cases, lipstick holders and metal novelties made to the specifications of the customer. *The American Perfumer*, 1934.

Sagamor Metal Goods Corporation manufactured compact cases, loose powder sifters, lipstick containers, and rouge and mascara cases. *The American Perfumer*, 1935.

Coty created holiday sets in 1930 and had a sensational advertising campaign. They contracted with authorized jewelry distributors and would reassure wholesalers that their products would be advertised to forty million readers in the most intensive newspaper campaign ever placed behind the Coty line. Coty would sell boxed compacts, lipstick gift sets, and compact and perfume combinations that would retail from $1.50 to $10.00. This would encourage wholesalers to purchase their products with the assurance that with all the advertising, their products would virtually sell themselves.

May, 1943.

Creations for the Christmas Trade

SOME charming packages created especially for the Christmas trade are presented in the photographs shown above. At the top, left, is Houbigant's attractive gift set of toilet water and face powder; next to it, in the center, are two of Coty's new holiday boxes, the set at the left containing face powder and toilet water and the other, powder, talc and a flacon of perfume; at the right is one of Volupté's latest style compacts in combination with a cigarette case and comb. In the middle row, left, is Dorothy Gray's new kit with six of her famous preparations; to the right, in the center,

is the charming "Colonielle" set of face powder, lipstick and compact, sponsored by Harry D. Koenig & Co.; at the extreme right are two of Pinaud's beautiful sets, the "Aida," containing perfume and face powder, and the "Vanity," with a double vanity and a bottle of perfume. In the bottom row, left, two of the famous "4711" sets of Ferd. Muelhens are shown, one containing eau de Cologne, talcum powder and bath salts, and the other, eau de Cologne, talcum powder and shaving cream; at the right is one of the colorful "Springtime in Paris" sets by Bourjois.

Essential Oil Review   *November, 1933*   441

Manufacturers created gift combinations for sale through the holidays. *The American Perfumer*, 1933.

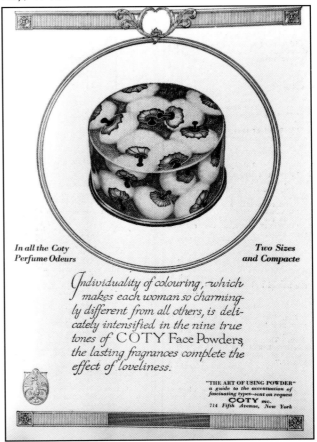

In all the Coty Perfume Odeurs

Two Sizes and Compacte

Individuality of colouring, which makes each woman so charmingly different from all others, is delicately intensified in the nine true tones of COTY Face Powders, the lasting fragrances complete the effect of loveliness.

"THE ART OF USING POWDER"
a guide to the accentuation of fascinating types—sent on request
COTY Inc.
714 Fifth Avenue, New York

Apollo Theatre.

The Charles of the Ritz line was developed for distribution in department stores and specialty shops in 1928 when John H. Hershman was appointed general manager and eventually president in 1930. A Charles of the Ritz salon in B. Altman & Co.'s store in New York opened in November of 1931. Open topped tables displayed Charles of the Ritz products. To the back of the grand reception room was an attractive manicure and treatment room with booths at one side and manicure tables at the other. Display cases all around the reception room encased the striking rose and gray packages of the Charles of the Ritz line.

Harriet Hubbard Ayer was born in Chicago in 1849. Ayer obtained a beauty formula in Europe and started her own cosmetic company in 1886 to support herself and her two daughters after a divorce. She sold the business, including the name, in 1906 to Vincent B. Thomas. His wife Lillian ran the business after his death from

Charles of the Ritz salon. *The American Perfumer*, 1931.

1918 to 1947. During this time, some of the items sold were Harriet Hubbard Ayer Face powder for about a dollar, lipstick, rouge, and eye brow pencils. In 1947, it was one of the largest cosmetic companies in the United States when it was sold to Lever Brothers. It changed hands to Nestle and then to Standard Metals Corporation in 1967.

The Elgin American Manufacturing Company produced a selection of wonderful enameled vanity compacts as well as watch/compact and cigarette/compact combinations. Many of the enameled compacts had a strong Art Deco influence that included bold geometric shapes in a variety of colors. Tango chains (with lipsticks attached by a chain to the compact) were another item manufactured by this company. Their slogan was "fit for a queen," and they advertised their specialty, an "Elginite enameled" compact front. The company acquired their name from the main factory located in Elgin, Illinois.

The **Lucerne Vanity**
in the Modern Manner!

Containing powder compact, rouge, lipstick and an extra compartment for bills or cigarettes, this Vanity Moderne retails for $7.50. At $10 you'll find the Lucerne—dressed for the evening—in exquisite chased metal!

◁
_____

The "Lucerne Vanity" by Terri. *Globe Theatre*, 1928.

Elgin American Manufacturers. Elgin, Illinois. *Fort Dearborn catalog*, 1929.

_____
▷

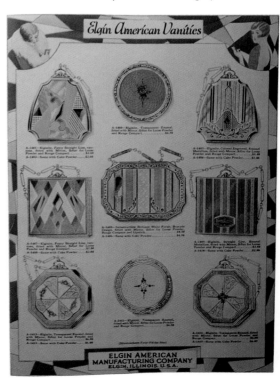

Vintage Compacts & Beauty Accessories

Coty created holiday sets in 1930 and had a sensational advertising campaign. They contracted with authorized jewelry distributors and would reassure wholesalers that their products would be advertised to forty million readers in the most intensive newspaper campaign ever placed behind the Coty line. Coty would sell boxed compacts, lipstick gift sets, and compact and perfume combinations that would retail from $1.50 to $10.00. This would encourage wholesalers to purchase their products with the assurance that with all the advertising, their products would virtually sell themselves.

May, 1943.

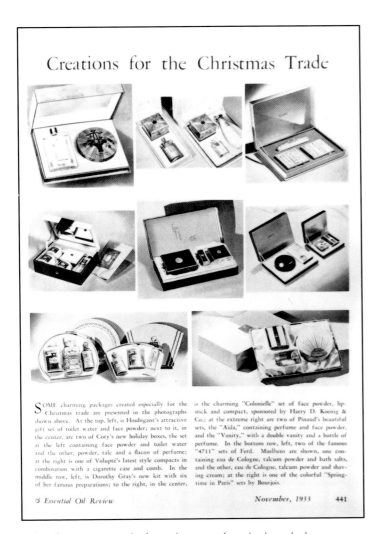

Creations for the Christmas Trade

SOME charming packages created especially for the Christmas trade are presented in the photographs shown above. At the top, left, is Houbigant's attractive gift set of toilet water and face powder; next to it, in the center, are two of Coty's new holiday boxes, the set at the left containing face powder and toilet water and the other, powder, talc and a flacon of perfume; at the right is one of Volupté's latest style compacts in combination with a cigarette case and comb. In the middle row, left, is Dorothy Gray's new kit with six of her famous preparations; to the right, in the center,

is the charming "Colonielle" set of face powder, lipstick and compact, sponsored by Harry D. Koenig & Co.; at the extreme right are two of Pinaud's beautiful sets, the "Aida," containing perfume and face powder, and the "Vanity," with a double vanity and a bottle of perfume. In the bottom row, left, two of the famous "4711" sets of Ferd. Muelhens are shown, one containing eau de Cologne, talcum powder and bath salts, and the other, eau de Cologne, talcum powder and shaving cream; at the right is one of the colorful "Springtime in Paris" sets by Bourjois.

The Essential Oil Review   *November, 1933*   441

Manufacturers created gift combinations for sale through the holidays. *The American Perfumer*, 1933.

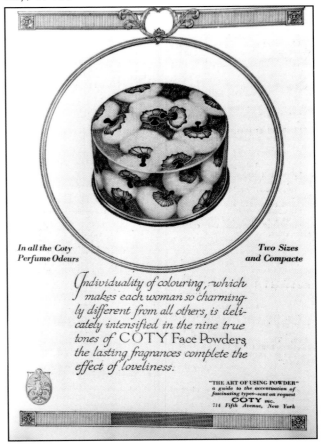

In all the Coty
Perfume Odeurs

Two Sizes
and Compacte

Individuality of colouring, which makes each woman so charmingly different from all others, is delicately intensified in the nine true tones of COTY Face Powders, the lasting fragrances complete the effect of loveliness.

"THE ART OF USING POWDER"
a guide to the accentuation of
fascinating types—sent on request
COTY INC.
714 Fifth Avenue, New York

Apollo Theatre.

The Charles of the Ritz line was developed for distribution in department stores and specialty shops in 1928 when John H. Hershman was appointed general manager and eventually president in 1930. A Charles of the Ritz salon in B. Altman & Co.'s store in New York opened in November of 1931. Open topped tables displayed Charles of the Ritz products. To the back of the grand reception room was an attractive manicure and treatment room with booths at one side and manicure tables at the other. Display cases all around the reception room encased the striking rose and gray packages of the Charles of the Ritz line.

Harriet Hubbard Ayer was born in Chicago in 1849. Ayer obtained a beauty formula in Europe and started her own cosmetic company in 1886 to support herself and her two daughters after a divorce. She sold the business, including the name, in 1906 to Vincent B. Thomas. His wife Lillian ran the business after his death from

1918 to 1947. During this time, some of the items sold were Harriet Hubbard Ayer Face powder for about a dollar, lipstick, rouge, and eye brow pencils. In 1947, it was one of the largest cosmetic companies in the United States when it was sold to Lever Brothers. It changed hands to Nestle and then to Standard Metals Corporation in 1967.

The Elgin American Manufacturing Company produced a selection of wonderful enameled vanity compacts as well as watch/compact and cigarette/compact combinations. Many of the enameled compacts had a strong Art Deco influence that included bold geometric shapes in a variety of colors. Tango chains (with lipsticks attached by a chain to the compact) were another item manufactured by this company. Their slogan was "fit for a queen," and they advertised their specialty, an "Elginite enameled" compact front. The company acquired their name from the main factory located in Elgin, Illinois.

Charles of the Ritz salon. *The American Perfumer*, 1931.

The "Lucerne Vanity" by Terri. *Globe Theatre*, 1928.

Elgin American Manufacturers. Elgin, Illinois. *Fort Dearborn catalog*, 1929.

The Lucerne Vanity
in the Modern Manner!

Containing powder compact, rouge, lipstick and an extra compartment for bills or cigarettes, this Vanity Moderne retails for $7.50. At $10 you'll find the Lucerne—dressed for the evening—in exquisite chased metal!

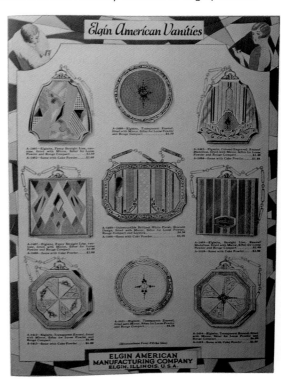

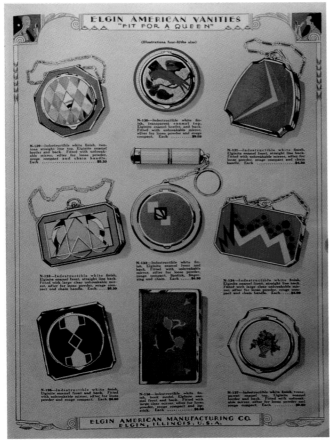

The ACB catalog, 1930.

By November of 1933, some charming packages were created especially for the Christmas trade. Holiday gift assortments added accessories such as perfumes, toilet water, talc, and lipsticks to be sold along with boxed face powder and compacts. This idea had been proven to work well during previous holiday sales. Included was Houbigant's attractive gift set of boxed face powder with a colorful flower basket on the lid, coupled with toilet water. Coty's new holiday boxes contained face powder, talc, and a flacon of perfume. Volupté's latest style of compacts was displayed in combination with cigarette cases and combs. Dorothy Gray's kit contained six of her famous preparations, and Colonielle, sponsored by Harry D. Koenig & Co., featured face powder, lipstick, and a compact. Pinaud's beautiful set included the "Aida," containing perfume and face powder, and the "Vanity," with a double vanity and a bottle of perfume. The "4711" sets by Ferd and Muelhens contained talcum powder, bath salts, and eau de Cologne. Bourjois launched its "Springtime in Paris" set which included eau de Cologne, talcum powder, and shaving cream.

That same year, Dr. Alice Carleton of the Department of Dermatology, Oxford, wrote an article for *The British Medical Journal* based upon the experimental use of Pond's Vanishing Cream. The analysis lasted from four to six weeks and consisted of testing forty women. One side of the face was rubbed with the cream, left overnight, and removed in the morning. More often than not, the results were favorable. Pond's jar was made by the Hazel-Atlas Glass Co.

Dorothy Gray engine-turned gold plated compact designed to resemble a wide brimmed ladies' hat. Circa: 1940s. *The Curiosity Shop.* $125-175.

A unique loose powder compact was added to the Dorothy Gray line in the thirties. The outer case was a four sectional, attractively shaded blue enamel. The powder was inserted from the back of the case and two springs meeting as the case is opened wide forced the powder through groove like openings. The Dorothy Gray double compact and lashlique, the powder compact, lipstick, powder and rouge compact were also new additions at that time. Boxed in pink velour paper with silver piping, they were lined with pink velvet. Another of Gray's compacts was available along with a box of face powder. Gray's additionally offered a swivel-type lipstick that was packaged in a silver and black metal case and available in eight shades.

———————

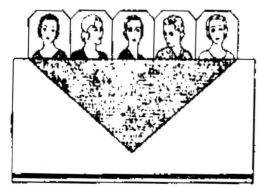

The Dorothy Gray Company designed this tinted fan for customer use in stores. When used like a color chart, it assisted in creating multiple sales. *The ACB catalog. The American Perfumer,* 1933.

D 91,000

Patent design for a cosmetic chart by Nathan Traub, Brooklyn, New York.

The Dorothy Gray Company launched an ingenious campaign in an effort to solve the make-up puzzle and promote additional sales of their products. A tinted fan assisted, when used like a color chart, to scientifically correct make-up ensembles. After examining about 20,000 faces and hiring a foremost color engineer to design the fan, it was possible to provide an accurate representation of skin tones. With a brand new color process, it determined slight differentiations between eight major skin types.

The fan was a determination of the tonal values of the skin. Each of the eight separate panels was accompanied by a smaller panel, bearing the correct shade of rouge and powder. All Dorothy Gray rouges were available with a corresponding lipstick, with the same name, such as "Tawny" rouge coupled with "Tawny" lipstick. This device made it easier to select Dorothy Gray cosmetics with precise color coordination.

The color fan was used by placing it against the throat, matching it with the correct skin tone. Then, the rouge and lipstick indicated by the nearest red panel of the fan gave the ideal make-up plan. These fans were available in shops, stores, and Dorothy Gray salons and helped promote multiple sales.

———————

The Sagamor Captive loose powder vanity was part of a striking window display campaign in New York. Designed on an entirely new principle patented by Sagamor, it held a generous supply of powder and an exceptionally heavy puff. *The American Perfumer,* 1931.

The Elizabeth Arden Salon at 25 Old Bond Street, London

The Elizabeth Arden Salon in London. Circa: 1930s. *The Quest of The Beautiful*.

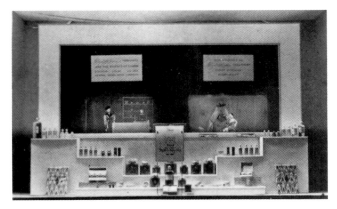

Elizabeth Arden's marionette window at Stern Brothers Department Store stopped traffic on busy 34th Street in New York. This clever marionette show featured Arden's products. *The American Perfumer*, 1934.

Top: Dorothy Gray goldtone loose powder compact with black enameled Savoir Faire raised mask, incised ribbons, mirror, 3" x 3¾". Bottom: Elizabeth Arden black enameled mask with deep powder well. 2½" x 3". *The Curiosity Shop*. Top, $80-100; bottom, $125-175.

Even the business of designing windows for cosmetic companies was a big undertaking in the 1930s. Dorothy Gray hired Lee Simonson, famous theatrical designer of stage settings who was celebrated for his Theatre Guild activities, to create a unique window for Gray. The design utilized two-story windows in the company's Fifth Avenue building as one advertising unit. It was the first time that anyone had attempted the difficult feat of carrying out a consecutive idea or design in windows on two separate stories. Schemes of decorations and ideas were top secret when these elaborate window designs were undertaken. An elaborate unveiling party was usually thrown when the work was finished.

In 1934, a novel method of advertising that evoked an enormously successful campaign was undertaken by Elizabeth Arden, Inc., stopping traffic on busy 34th Street in New York. Through the efforts of this ingenious and unusual compact and toiletry advertising campaign, the company utilized a large window front of the salon at Stern Brothers Department Store by operating a clever marionette show featuring Arden's products. While the mechanics of the operation were complicated, the idea was simple: the upper portion was divided into two sections; behind the window of the first section, a well dressed marionette in shopping mode demonstrated the consumer enthusiastically purchasing Arden products in the store. The second window showed her gingerly applying them in the 'privacy' of her boudoir. At the

bottom, a showcase and shelving featured a beautiful assortment of Arden's compacts, powders, creams, and toiletries. Potential customers were fascinated by the animation of the marionette show during the week it was in operation. It boosted sales tremendously and word of mouth advertising helped to make the Arden name even more famous.

Arden also created some charming bath sets made to harmonize with the powder box, packaged in a blue box with yellow trimmings. Another unique design for Arden in 1933 was "Velva Beauty Film" for the legs. Available in a tube, the purpose of the product was to act as a covering for skin blemishes.

The Quest of the Beautiful was a charming beauty booklet produced in 1931, showcasing Arden's products. With locations in London, New York, Berlin, Paris, Madrid, and Rome, her treatments included muscle strapping and skin toning. The original Arden salon was in New York on Fifth Avenue and was a rendezvous place for prominent society and stage beauties. Other salons were located in busy cities like Los Angeles, Chicago, and Miami Beach. Cleansing, nourishing, toning, and tightening were fundamentals of the Arden philosophy. She created the Elizabeth Arden Patter, the unusual looking small disk shaped object on a long stick that was presumed to tone the muscles of the face and neck.

The Arden Venetian Preparations were produced in private laboratories under supervision. The formulas were developed during her many years of experience as a specialist in skin treatment. She was the first authority to condemn the use of an all-purpose cream and to develop her complete group of specialized preparations to fulfill every beauty need and correct faults of the skin. Each of the assistants in her salons was trained under her personal supervision.

Arden promoted her Illusion powder box packaged with Amoretta rouge and evening powder. She also offered Venetian Flower Powder that was delicately perfumed and was advertised not to give the facial skin that uncomfortable drawn feeling. It sold for $1.75 and was available in several shades to match skin tone. Other powders available were Poudre D'illusion and Venetian Poudre De Soir. The Arden line also consisted of rouge, lip pastes and sticks, and compacts.

The compacts offered by Elizabeth Arden were the Petite O'Boy Compact, Ardenette, Double Ardenette, Venetian Petite, and the Venetian Carino Compact. The Petite O'Boy was a double flat powder/rouge combination in a thin, round, goldtone chased case with a mirror and two puffs. The case was available in a single design containing only powder or rouge. They sold for $2.50 each. The Ardenette was octagonal and engine turned and could carry the customer's favorite loose powder. Available in gold or black and silver, it sold from $3.00 to $4.00. The Double Ardenette also contained rouge and had an unbreakable chromium mirror. A hammered goldtone case in a dainty size was called the Venetian Petite.

The Venetian Carino was a beautiful box of highly polished goldtone that was fitted with a small shield area for a monogram. Inside the box was a puff, mirror, and a tablet of powder or rouge. It sold for $1.25.

One of the more unusual items presented by Arden was a DeLuxe Chin Strap that wrapped around the chin to the

IN ELIZABETH ARDEN's Exercise Department, you will be guided by a competent director who appreciates your problem even before you do yourself. Every movement will do something definitely just for *you*. You will learn how to win the firm, slender waist of youth, how to straighten your shoulders, and to carry your head with the gallant charm which is your birthright. To be sure of an appointment at the hour you prefer, please telephone — Plaza 5847.

Elizabeth Arden's Venetian Toilet Preparations are on sale at the smart shops everywhere

ELIZABETH ARDEN
673 FIFTH AVENUE, NEW YORK

	Boston	Philadelphia	Chicago	Detroit	
	San Francisco	Los Angeles	Atlantic City	Washington	
LONDON		BERLIN	PARIS	MADRID	ROME

[34]

Some of the more unusual items presented by Elizabeth Arden were a DeLuxe Chin Strap and The Venetian Forehead Strap. All devices could be used in conjunction with the Venetian Patter. *Avon Theatre.*

Richard Hudnut, Elizabeth Arden, and Dorothy Gray printed booklets containing instructions for a regime of cleansing and protecting combined with the use of their products.

Elizabeth Arden's "Ardena Invisible veil" powder box. 2½" dia. *The Curiosity Shop*. $15-25.

top of the head. It was made of flesh colored satin with an inner lining for astringent herbs which were to aid and invigorate relaxed muscles. It was to be worn every day for fifteen minutes and sold for ten dollars. The Venetian Forehead Strap and Puffy Eye Strap were two other devices that could be used in conjunction with the Elizabeth Arden Venetian Patter.

During the holiday season, Helena Rubinstein introduced a new deluxe powder jar that attracted wide spread attention because of its beautiful design. The jar, quite different from those on the market at the time, was made of a highly lustrous and ornamental silver crystal glass. The screw top cover accommodated a black plastic rim. Rubinstein created an "automatic" lipstick enclosed in a novel case which allows opening and closing with one light pressure of the thumb, and could be applied with the use of one hand. In a clever silver tone case, it was available in three French shades.

Richard Hudnut was a hugely popular compact manufacturer with a number of successful compact and beauty products available in the early part of this century. The company owned the famous DuBarry Success School where the beauty preparations were used, and the Richard Hudnut Salon on Fifth Avenue in New York. One of their prestigious addresses was in Paris. The company also sold products in Germany. Hudnut wrote several helpful beauty books which gave an additional boost to his sales. Titles included: *Be a DuBarry Beauty* and *The Lovely Skin You Can Have*. These charming mini books included tips, advice, product ideas, and prices. Hudnut advertised the powder "to be as kind as candlelight to your complexion." One of the company's offerings was a powder and rouge combination with a mirror to carry in the purse. It cost one dollar and was available in the same shades as DuBarry Lipsticks.

A famous preparation by Hudnut was the Three Flowers series. The company suggested cleansing, nourishing, finishing and protecting which included use of the Three Flowers Vanishing Cream, Skin and Tissue Builder, Cleansing Cream, and fluffing with powder "to cling evenly and softly for hours, smoothing the surface of the skin." To the elegant woman, Hudnut claimed, powder was not make-up, but more an atmosphere, a breath of added softness on her satiny skin. Hudnut face powder was smooth and of the finest ingredients, the texture and color made to blend inconspicuously with each complexion. Also recommended was both a day and evening powder. The offerings were Gardenia, Deauville, and DuBarry scents. Face powders were priced from seventy-five cents to three dollars. The Three Flowers Compact was fifty cents.

The New York manufacturer attractively packaged an atomizer in a box typical of the other items of the Hudnut line. The outer covering was mottled brown and orange. A loose powder vanity was also added which had a decorative case of black and buff with an ornamental design in silver tone.

———— •—•—• ————

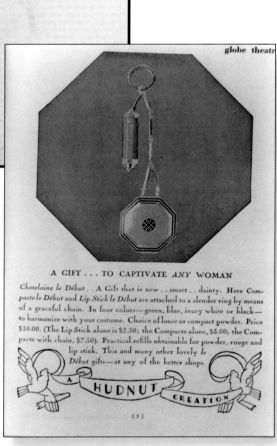

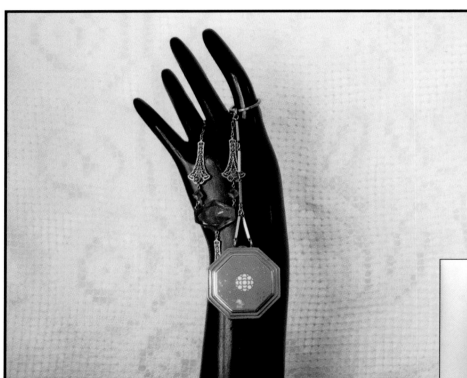

Richard Hudnut's *le Debut*, an octagon shaped vanity compact, enameled blue with celestial design. This compact was available in four colors—green, blue, ivory, or black. The compact with finger ring chain sold for $7.50. 2" dia. Circa: 1920. Shown open, powder and rouge compartments with puffs are revealed, separated by a mirror. *The Curiosity Shop.* $150-225.

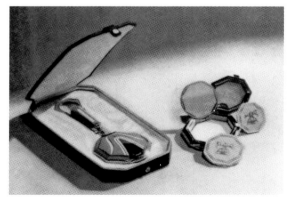

"Le Debut" compact and lipstick ensemble by Richard Hudnut. *The American Perfumer,* 1931.

"Chatelaine le Debut" by Richard Hudnut. Compact, finger ring chain, and lipstick sold for ten dollars. *Globe Theatre,* 1928.

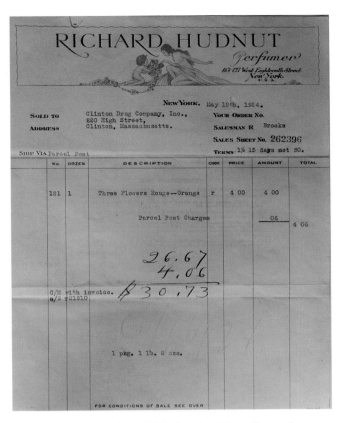

Original invoice from Richard Hudnut for "Three Flowers" rouge. 1924.

Richard Hudnut.

"Du Barry" cosmetics by Richard Hudnut.

Powder boxes by Richard Hudnut.

A German Richard Hudnut window screen. 1930.

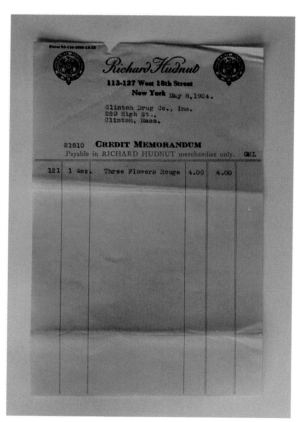

Richard Hudnut invoice for "Three Flowers" cosmetics.
1924.

Hudnut also produced an unusual doll faced hand mirror that included a lipstick tube concealed in the handle. Probably made of composition or an early plastic, details include black and cream colored painting and a floral motif. It has gold plated brass accents, marked "DuBarry."

Loose powder compacts were popular at this time and Primrose House, Inc. of New York presented a cherry red enameled compact/rouge combination targeting the younger customer for summer. Prince Matchabelli also released a loose powder compact line. The compartment for the powder was filled by pushing back the small slide. To secure the powder when desired, this compartment was slid forward and sufficient powder for use was deposited in the groove in the forefront of the compact. The cover design was in keeping with the other Matchabelli cases, which are black and gold with the Matchabelli crown in gold on a black background.

A powder jar known as "Poudre des perles" was added to the Kathleen Mary Quinlan product line in 1931. It was a round glass jar with a decorative plastic screw top. The jar was packaged in a black box lined with pink. A loose powder compact of Quinlan's provided powder by turning the bottom of the case until powder sufficient for use was sifted through the openings.

Hand mirror/lipstick combination with raised doll face, signed "DuBarry." 3" x 6". *Author's Collection*. $125-175.

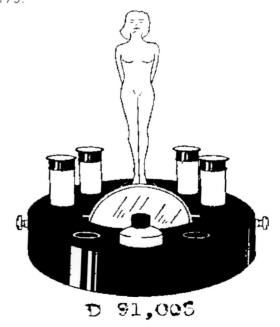

Patent design for an advertising display stand by James L. Younghusband, Chicago, Illinois.

V. Vivaudou's lipstick was presented in a metal case of silver and jade in five indelible shades. Cheramy, Inc., New York, well known for its popular "April Showers" line, also promoted their specialty "Mayflowers" line, a bouquet fragrance that included a toilet water and face powder. Cara Nome, sponsored by the United Drug Co., Boston, offered a smart new face powder package of olive shade, trimmed and tied with a blue ribbon wrapped in cellulose.

Yardley released a product in the fall of 1934. An indelible lipstick, it was offered to the trade with a color selector counter display stand. Cases were platinum finished and ten sided, giving them an interesting streamlined effect. Five shades in the usual popular range of colors were available. The display stand was given to the dealer with an order of sufficient size.

Volupté was a large volume compact manufacturer that also sold pill boxes, cigarette cases, carryalls, and atomizers. A firm believer in advertising and promotion, the company had a radio quiz show on Thursday evenings called *The Better Half*. In the late Forties and early Fifties, as advertised in *Vogue*, they offered a free illustrated booklet entitled *Collector's Items by Volupté*. It described how to decorate your home with compacts, stating that fashionable women and Hollywood stars collected them. Some of the items in the series included novelty and figural items in the shapes of other objects, for instance, a purse, piano, and a vanity table.

As part of this series, Volupté manufactured a metal compact with raised white and black enameled keys on a keyboard, made to resemble a legless grand piano. A beautiful scalloped edged compact designed to resemble a vanity table with collapsible legs, called the "Petite Boudoir," was a perfect miniature of the carved golden dressing table that Marie Antoinette used her bed chamber. In the late forties, Rita Hayworth was hired by the manufacturer to promote the "Lucky Purse" during the time that she starred in the Columbia motion picture *Carmen*. This compact was in the shape of a purse and came with a textured brushed gold finish, a smooth gilt finish, and other details sometimes including a wrist chain made to resemble a purse strap. Dorothy Lamour, during her role in *The Lucky Stiff* by United Artists, appeared in advertisements for the "Lucky Purse." The "Swinglok," although non-figural, was also a part of the series. This square, textured compact has a decorative bar that opens and closes with a flip of the finger.

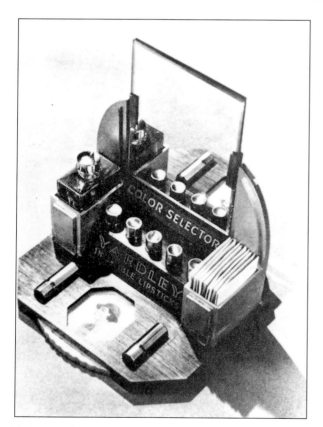

Yardley's indelible lipstick with a color selector counter display stand used by shop owners in 1934. *The American Perfumer.*

Woman's Home Companion, September 1942.

Silver powder case, signed "Alpacca." 2¾" x 2¾". *Courtesy of Walter Kitik.* $125-200.

Encharma
Cold Cream Complexion Powder

The Latest Luxor Creation!

THE PUREST of cold creams, the softest, the most delightful of powders, unite their benefits to the skin in this exquisite new Luxor Requisite. And it stays on so enduringly long — until removed! In stunning *oval* box, with velvety puff enclosed. Sold everywhere.

LUXOR Limited
Perfumers
PARIS   CHICAGO   NEW YORK

Luxor

TOILET REQUISITES
of ENDURING CHARM

Luxor Rouge Parfait—the most widely used in America—and exquisite, clinging Luxor Complexion Powder find perfect setting and easy accessibility in this, the only gold-plated, thin duo compact selling for $1.50 today.

A Liberal Sample—Free!

Present this advertisement to any dealer in Greater New York and receive an exquisite miniature of generous size. free. If dealer cannot supply you, mail ad to Luxor, Ltd., 1355 West 31st Street, Chicago, Ill.

Apollo Theatre, 1924.

hammerstein's theatre

ITS COLOR CHANGES . . .
to blend with your complexion
TANGEE

Based on a marvelous color principle, Tangee changes as you put it on . . . and blends perfectly with your individual complexion, whether blonde, brunette or titian.

For Tangee gives a natural glow without thickness or substance . . . permanent with never a trace of grease or smear. Unlike other lipsticks, Tangee has a solidified cream base . . . it not only beautifies but actually soothes and heals. *There is only one TANGEE. Be sure you see the name TANGEE on the package.*

The Geo. W. Luft Co., 417 Fifth Ave., New York

Tangee Lipstick $1. Tangee Rouge Compact 75¢. Tangee Créme Rouge $1. The new Tangee Powder $1. Tangee Day Cream $1. Tangee Night Cream $1. Tangee Cosmetic for the eyelashes and eyebrows $1.

[9]

Hammerstein's Theatre Program.

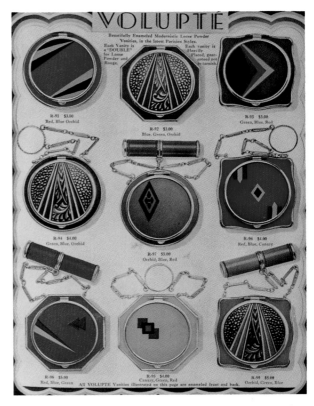

VOLUPTÉ

Beautifully Enameled Modernistic Loose Powder Vanities, in the Latest Parisian Styles.
Each Vanity is a "DOUBLE" for Loose Powder and Rouge.   Each vanity is Heavily Plated, guaranteed not to tarnish.

R-91 $3.00
Red, Blue Orchid

R-92 $3.00
Blue, Green, Orchid

R-93 $3.00
Green, Blue, Red

R-94 $4.00
Green, Blue, Orchid

R-97 $5.00
Orchid, Blue, Red

R-96 $4.00
Red, Blue, Canary

R-98 $5.00
Red, Blue, Green

R-95 $4.00
Canary, Green, Red

R-99 $5.00
Orchid, Green, Blue

ALL VOLUPTÉ Vanities illustrated on this page are enameled front and back.

Volupté Art Deco inspired enameled compacts, some with tango chains and finger ring attachments. *The ACB catalog,* 1930.

Tangee advertisement.

Delineator, 1917.

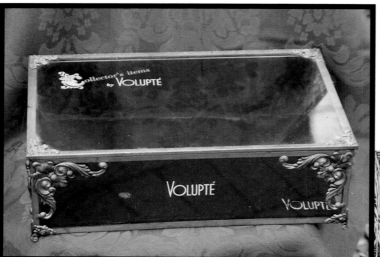

Volupté glass and brass store presentation case. *Lori Landgrebe Antiques.* $80-120.

"Elmo" eye shadow. 1" x 1½". *The Curiosity Shop.* $15-35.

Royalty souvenir group. At top: their majesties King George VI and Queen Elizabeth in Bakelite, dated 1937. $125-175. Second row left: Pygmalion, made in England, $75-125. Right: manufactured by Mascot. $75-125. Third row left: the Queen laughing during her coronation, made in Great Britain by Mascot in 1953. $75-125. Right: the Queen with Prince Philip is a transfer made by Stratton. $75-125. All are 3" dia.
From The Collection of Joan Orlen, Photograph by Steven Freeman Photography.

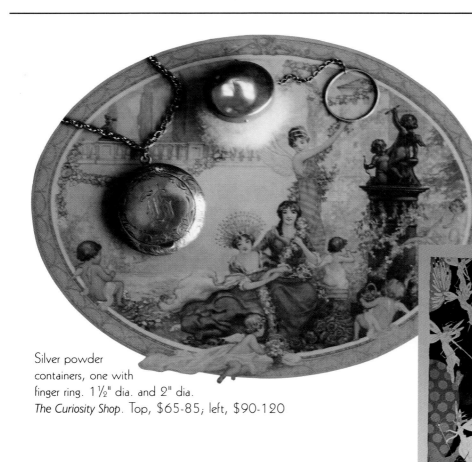

Silver powder
containers, one with
finger ring. 1½" dia. and 2" dia.
The Curiosity Shop. Top, $65-85; left, $90-120

Woman's Home Companion, February
1918.

"Djer-Kiss" perfume and powder gift set in elaborate presentation box. Glass containers are
used for perfume and cologne, detailed powder box. *The Curiosity Shop.* $125-175.

"Djer-Kiss" silvertone vanity case with raised fairies and nymphs, powder and rouge compartments. Circa: 1920s. 2½" x 2½". *The Curiosity Shop*. $120-160.

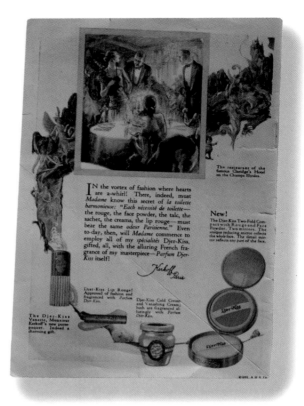

1923.

The "Venus-Ray," a compact with a light with lipstick refill case and perfume vial. *November, 1947.*

The Ladies Home Journal, September, 1923.

A make-up color chart by Elizabeth Post.

1918.

Unsigned lightly enameled octagon shaped compact with adjustable wrist chain. 4" x 4". *The Curiosity Shop*. $125-175.

Vintage Compacts & Beauty Accessories

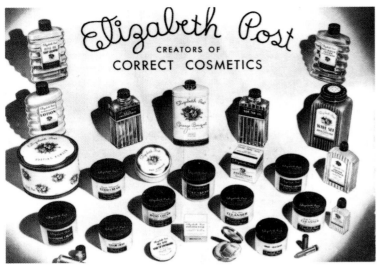

Cosmetic selections by Elizabeth Post.

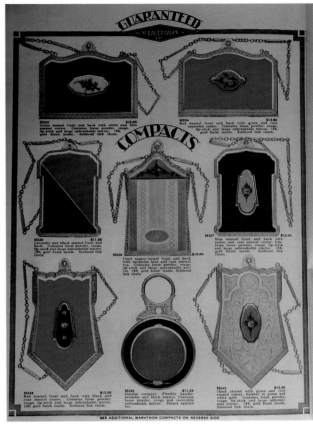

Aisenstein and Gordon catalog, 1929.

The Wadsworth *Pandora* black velvet carryall sling. Shown open, the taffeta lined black velvet sack unveils a cylinder carryall with dual access. The puff has the "Wadsworth" logo and the interior reveals a clear plastic comb, lipstick, powder cavity, and mirror. Circa: 1952. *The Curiosity Shop*. $225-300.

The Evans Company reveals a selection of cleverly enameled compacts with flexible handles and finger rings in the $4.25 to $9.00 wholesale price range. *Aisenstein and Gordon catalog, 1929.*

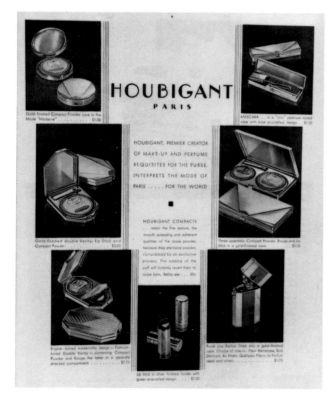

The Ladies Home Journal, 1931.

Houbigant "Floral Basket" motif powder boxes, signed "Quelques Fleurs." 3" to 3½" by 1" to 1½" deep, Paris. *The Curiosity Shop.* $40-60 each.

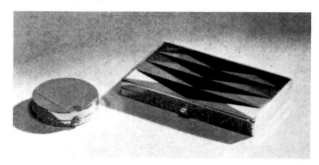

Houbigant's rouge at left, and triple compact that contains lipstick, rouge, and "Quelques Fleurs" powder. *The American Perfumer,* 1931.

Bourjois, Inc., of New York displays their triple compact for the "Evening in Paris" cosmetic line. *The American Perfumer,* 1931.

ULTRA SMART VANITY SETS

Manufacturers combined compacts in pre-packaged sets
with lipsticks, combs, and rouge for greater customer appeal.
C P & S catalog, 1930.

Houbigant's "Flower Basket" Compact

Houbigant, Inc., New York, has brought out
a new double compact in a scratch-proof, chromium finished case with a pearl gray top embellished
in color with the Houbigant "flower basket." The
case is light in weight and convenient, and contains
the company's famous "dull finish" face powder.

Houbigant's "Flower Basket" double compact with a scratch-
proof, chromium finished case. *The American Perfumer*, 1934.

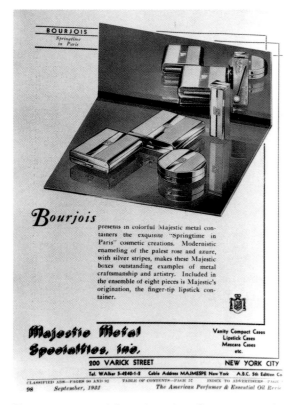

The Majestic Metal Specialties, Inc. Company manufactured the metal containers for the Bourjois "Springtime in
Paris" line. *The American Perfumer*, 1932.

Making sure that packaging appealed to the intended consumer
was of critical importance. Manufacturers referred to labels as
"the personality of the package."

The Foster Blue Book, 1925-26.

Rex Fifth Avenue, ivory colored vinyl flapjack cases with multicolored floral sprays. 1940s. 4½" dia. $40-50 each.

An early advertisement for Johnson's baby powder depicts a young girl powdering her face. This photograph entitled "Finishing Touches" was a free gift with a purchase. Circa: 1900.

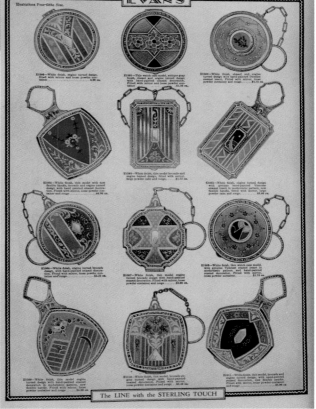

The Evans Company advertises a variety of delicately enameled compacts in 1929. *Aisenstein and Gordon catalog.*

The American Perfumer, 1931.

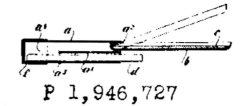

P 1,946,727

Store stock face powder boxes from Ponds. 2½" dia.
The Curiosity Shop. $5-10 each.

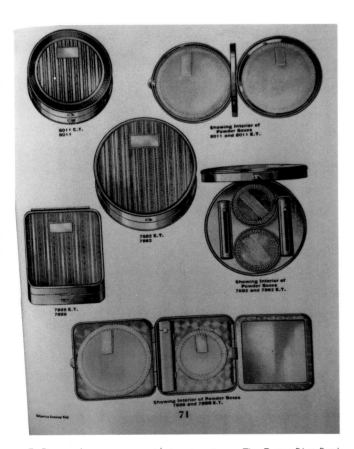

F&B powder compacts with interior views. *The Foster Blue Book*, 1925-26.

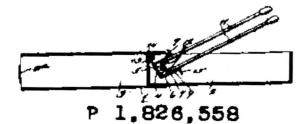

P 1,826,558

The Ladies Home Journal, 1921.

The Ladies Home Journal, October, 1919.

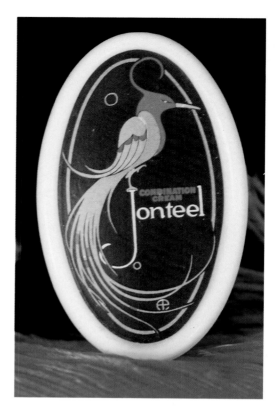

Jonteel combination cream in heavy milk glass container. *The Curiosity Shop*. $50-75.

Artist's rendering of ornate vanity case designed for Bliss, circa: 1910. *Courtesy of The Napier Company.*

The Jewelers' Circular, February, 1920.

Vintage Compacts & Beauty Accessories

Cohan and Harris Theatre.

A sample of Freeman's face powder by the Freeman Perfume Company, Cincinnati, Ohio. Circa: 1910. *The Curiosity Shop.* $25-40.

Violet talcum powder sample, Byron C. Gould, Inc., New York, circa: 1910. *The Curiosity Shop.* $25-40.

LaBlache face powder advertisement. *Theatre Magazine*, 1924.

The treacherous trail to the MODERN

FULL of pitfalls. That is a good way to describe the trail that the cosmetician must follow when he wishes to *modernize* his containers.

One danger is that the containers will turn out to be "modernistic" instead of modern, "tricky" instead of authentic and compelling. Again, modern containers must gain rather than lose in utility and display value. They must deserve and win thousands of votes from practical women everywhere.

It is the business of the Scovill Manufacturing Company, in designing and manufacturing modern containers for cosmeticians, to avoid all of the pitfalls so far as specialized skill and intensive experience can avoid them. Ever since the modern became an almost essential factor in package and container design, our specialists have been concerned almost daily in combining the modern with the useful and practical.

Above are illustrated some of the containers for the "Lanchère" line manufactured by Scovill for *Marshall Field & Company*. They are good

examples of the skill with which Scovill designers bring practical expression and manufacturing economy to the customer's requirements.

In artistic understanding, expressed economically in terms of the finest workmanship, Scovill offers to cosmeticians a unique service in the design and manufacture of containers. An opportunity to study your problems will be welcomed.

Scovill
SCOVILL MANUFACTURING COMPANY
WATERBURY   CONNECTICUT
New York, Philadelphia, Boston, Providence, Chicago, Syracuse, Detroit, Cleveland, Cincinnati, Atlanta, San Francisco, Los Angeles. In Europe: The Hague, Holland.

66   *August, 1931*   *The American Perfumer*

The American Perfumer, 1931.

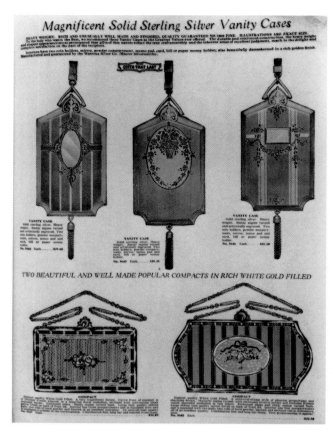

The Foster Blue Book, 1925-26.

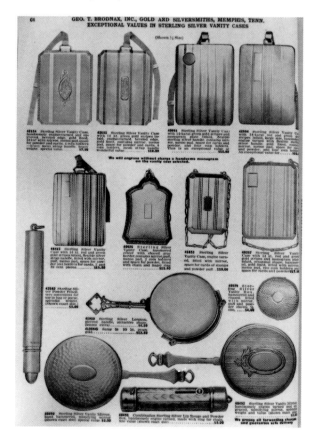

George T. Brodnax, Inc.

The American Perfumer, 1932.

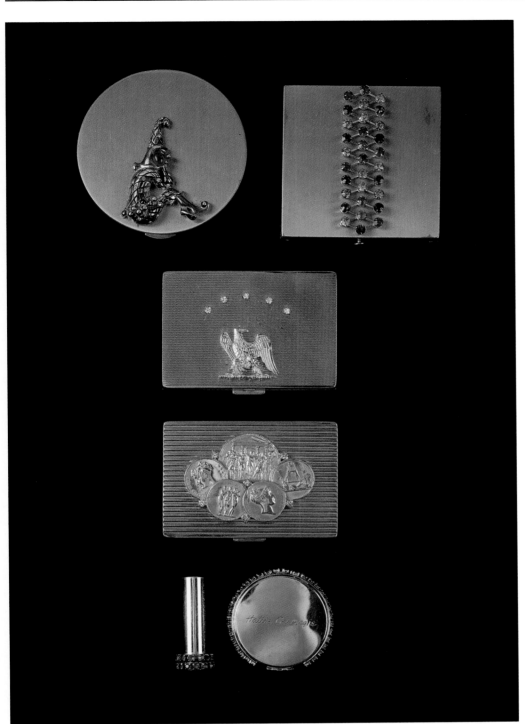

Manufacturers joined costume jewelry designers to create interesting faux jeweled compacts. Top row left is a harlequin, 3½" dia, $200-300; right is 3" x 3", $150-200, both are signed "Eisenberg." The eagle and coin motif compacts measure 3½" x 2½", $90-150 each; the round powder and lipstick receptacle set is 2", $75-125 set. All four are signed "Hattie Carnegie." *From The Collection of Joan Orlen, Photograph by Steven Freeman Photography.*

New Amsterdam Theatre.

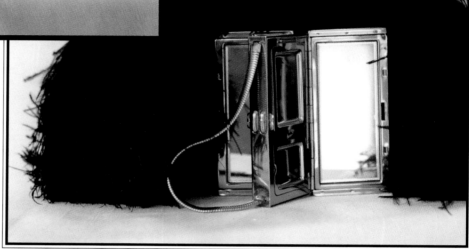

Wadsworth "Ball and Chain" in presentation box. Goldtone lipstick tube attached by linked chain to round powder compact with plastic interior and mirror. 2" dia. *Lori Landgrebe Antiques*. $125-175.

A cylinder carryall with dual access, flexible metal snake chain. Compartments for powder, rouge, trinkets, and mirrors. 2½" x 4½". *The Curiosity Shop*. $150-225.

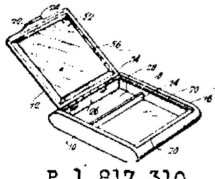

P 1,817,310

Dorothy Gray make-up/travel kit that includes salon face powder, orange flower skin lotion, dry skin cleanser, foundation cream, and dry skin mixture. These kits were given catchy names like "Cabana Case," "Freshen-Up Kit," and "Treasurette." *The Curiosity Shop*. $100-150.

Beauty boxes and make-up kits were first created for a surprising reason. Their primary function was to acquaint the customer with as many of the manufacturer's powders and preparations as possible, resulting in many ingenious innovations for increased sales.

The travel theme has been one of the most popular exploitations of this idea. Cruise and Pullman kits, cabin cases, weekend beauty boxes, and many others with catchy names such as "Cabana Case," "Tripkit," "Treasurette," "Hat-Box," etc., could fill the beauty requirements of every phase of travel. A clever name for the make-up kit, in keeping with the specific functions of the beauty case, gave it significance and lifted it above the rank and file of others.

Similar to luggage, most were elaborately constructed, complete enough to accommodate the traveler for anything from a week-end jaunt to a year-round trip. Generally constructed of wood and covered with leather, many have additional compartments for small clothing and for additional toilet necessities—from the toothbrush on up. They ranged in price from around five dollars for the smaller week-end variety to as much as one hundred and fifty dollars for the most luxurious.

Lucien Lelong.

Lelong's Beauty box.
The American Perfumer,
1931.

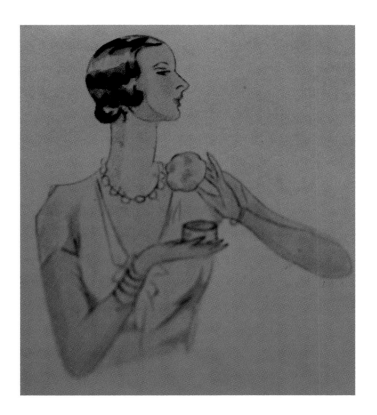

Another more obvious method of selling an assembled group of toiletries had been in the form of a get-acquainted package. These might have been used for traveling too, but that use was not always emphasized. Sometimes they were very modest, containing extremely miniature packages, and were sold at a nominal price. Even the more pretentious ones were usually priced lower than the total cost of the individual items if sold separately. The method was a sound one and undoubtedly accomplished the purpose of acquainting the customer with one or more items which may not have interested them particularly otherwise, but which, upon use, provided sufficient interest to induce future purchases of larger sizes. To prevent regular customers of a certain product from taking advantage of the savings on such an acquaintance kit, a company restricted sales to those who had never used the merchandise previously. This tactic had the advantage of making those who were thus being introduced to the line by the purchase feel that this was a special privilege being extended to them. The items belonging to this group went by the names of "Invitation Kit," "Minute Make-Up Kit," and "Introduction Kit."

One type of presentation often directed its appeal to the very busy woman on the basis of its convenience for quick but thorough make-up, and its easy portability to the office or club. Business women in the thirties who led a life of rapidly successive appointments found these little beauty boxes handy to keep in their desk drawers for those occasions when a dinner engagement followed too closely on business hours, or when they wished to "brighten up" during lunch time or at the energy let-down period in mid-afternoon.

College girls, notorious for their hectic way of life, found that these kits simplified their beauty routine. They were ideal for the school gymnasium locker or for a facial going-over before dashing from swimming class to mathematics. Similarly, the sportswoman, or any woman who led a life largely outside of the home, favored an unobtrusive yet complete package for her beauty equipment. These compact kits often had such inviting and suggestive names as "Freshen-Up Kit," or "Pick-Me-Up Kit." Quite frequently, these were informal and practical. Those covered or lined with washable fabrics which imitated linen and gingham had a fresh, summery appearance which was most appealing to the vacationer.

Billie Burke Beauty Box, depicting a boy and girl in petitpoint. 3" x 6½" x 2" deep. *From The Collection of Joan Orlen, Photograph by Steven Freeman Photography.* Very rare.

Dorothy Gray's make-up kit contained salon face powder, dry skin cleanser, make-up foundation cream, a special dry skin mixture, and orange flower skin lotion. Packaged in an attractive red handled box, it had a pull out mirror.

Elizabeth Arden had several travel cases available in the early 1930s. One of the more expensive cases sold for one hundred dollars and had creams and lotions in aluminum containers. In the box were trays, filled with powders and toiletries, that could slide open. A large mirror was included. The case was made of leather, black cobra, or tan suede alligator. The containers were devised to hold generous quantities.

The Arden Travel Case is of black Moroccan grain designed to match luggage with a gilt lock and key. The Travel Case contained Venetian Cleansing and Pore Cream, Venetian Orange Skin Food, tonics, astringent, lotion, hand cream, flower powder, Muscle Oil, cleansing tissues and tooth brush, and sold for thirty dollars. The Boudoir Beauty Box was suitable for a month of travel and sold for eighteen dollars. Arden's Bijou Beauty Box contained important preparations that were used every day, with finishing touches such as powder, eyebrow pencil and brush. Perfect for a small vanity table or motor trunk, it was nine dollars. The Week-End Beauty Box sold for $3.85. Ready to be tucked into an overnight bag or for short visits, it carried a modest variety of facial treatments along with samples.

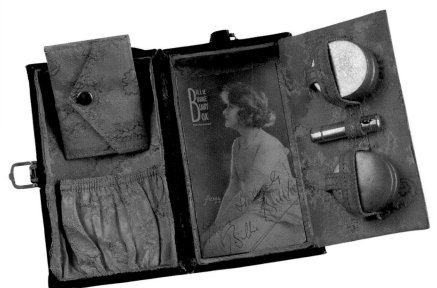

Shown open, a photograph of Billie Burke is revealed, along with cosmetic receptacles and lipstick, original lining, and a change purse. The mirror is exposed by flipping a piece of the fabric interior behind the cosmetics. *From The Collection of Joan Orlen, Photograph by Steven Freeman Photography.*

Asprey of London produced a variety of attractive cases in the 1920s, calling them modern fitted suitcases, dressing cases, and "compactus" cases. In business since the late 1700s, their high quality kits included a wide range of necessities including brushes, combs, and manicure sets as well as powder and perfume containers. Made from Moroccan leather, crocodile, and seal, many of these handsome cases had mirrors, pockets, and special compartments for trinkets.

A rather rare and unusual make-up kit came equipped with a Brownie camera and celluloid compact and rouge container in a lockable case. Also included was a lipstick and comb as the case was designed for primping before a photograph was taken.

Lucien Lelong, who was noted for his perfumes, also endorsed products for the beauty trade. He designed a beauty box in the 1930s that contained a tray accommodating perfume, rouge, eye pencil, cosmetique, and lipstick. The tray fitted in the top of the container while beneath it was the powder. A substantial mirror was contained under the lid. The box was decorated in various colored enamels, black, jade, and pink, with the characteristic Lelong trimmings and trademark on the top of the receptacle.

Other types of cases were designed for the beach enthusiast. These beach boxes and bags were usually constructed of rubber or some other hardy material and closed with a zipper which was much easier for wet hands to cope with than keys and locks. The items were beach appropriate and included standards like sunburn creams, oils, and ointments, perhaps a hair lotion to keep the hair from getting dried out, suntan face powder, suntan make-up, and leg make-up. As clever and attractive as these beach gadgets were, the manu-

facturer had to realize that the market was limited not only seasonally, but also in customer appeal. Not every person could afford more than one kit that was adjusted to all occasions.

Manufacturers took beauty box and make-up kit creating very seriously. If they were designing for the inveterate traveler, who would continually go on round-the-world cruises, they would build a sea-worthy case that would last the trip and not collapse in mid-Mediterranean. Armed with their specifications, there would be extensive consultations with proven luggage manufacturers. There, the beauty box producer would learn the secrets of properly ageing woods, the best choice of wood for the purpose, how to prevent warping, lock durability and security, and all that was needed to know to make satisfactory and sturdy beauty boxes.

Sometimes, the boxes needed not to be constructed for the same permanence as the luggage, made either of light wood or enamelled metal. If it was to be the type of case that would be packed rather than carried, a fine paper box manufacturer would be consulted in order to design an attractive encasement.

When designing and manufacturing travel and make-up kits, appropriate adjustments had to be made. An attractive dressing table con-

Make-up kit designers studied luggage manufacturer's procedures to make sturdy beauty boxes for inveterate travelers.

tainer was not necessarily a suitable travel container. It had to be water and dust resistant as well as non-leaking. Bottles with double protection caps were used. Powders were kept in screw cap jars or tins. Creams and ointments were more desirable in tubes than jars. Hardy, rather than dainty packages withstood the wear and tear of travel better.

Manufacturers adjusted the number of preparations to the purpose of the kit. Habitual travelers required a larger assortment of toiletries than the vacationer. In turn, the vacationer required more items than the weekender, but an overnight guest had fewer requirements than any of the others. A large assortment of preparations in travel-sized packages made it possible to accomplish certain fundamental changes to suit each individual purchaser. Basic items would include toiletries for cleansing and refreshing, but make-up items like powders, rouge, lipstick, and others were added, as well as bath and sun-tan preparations, in accordance to the needs of the prospective user and the simplicity or complexity desired.

Colorful coverings were used for one season kits. However, if a make-up case was designed for continual year-round use, then color choices were confined to more sober ones such as dark blue, dark green, brown, or black.

Fabrics, too, depended on the amount of time the kit was expected to be in use. Real leather was most durable for exclusive make-up kit construction, but some fine imitation leathers were also used. Washable fabrics also ranked high in practicality. Cloth or paper were least durable but satisfactory if durability was not a feature of the case.

A compact case with a little extra room allowance for accessories was a big hit. This was often accomplished by raising some packages and letting them rest on the shoulders of the case, instead of flatly on the bottom of the case. Odds and ends such as a toothbrush, comb, hairpins, handkerchiefs, etc., were tucked into those little nooks and crannies, adding to convenience, or pockets were made in the side or in the cover of the box for these sundries.

Fine leather cosmetic overnight case with adjustable strap and snap closure. 4½" x 5½". *Author's Collection.* $225-275.

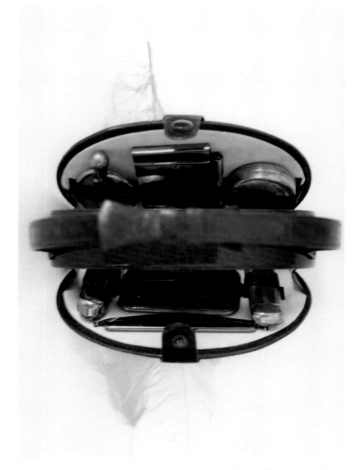

Shown open revealing travel safe containers for perfume, lipstick, powder, and pills. Also, notepad with pencil, comb, and mirror.

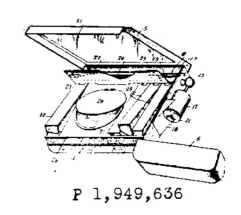

P 1,949,636

Elizabeth Arden's travel case with aluminum containers sold for $100.
The Quest of The Beautiful.

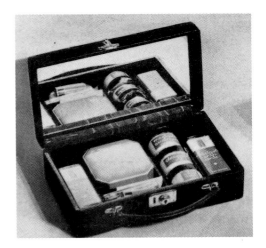

The American Perfumer, 1934.

The American Perfumer, 1934.

The American Perfumer, 1934.

A rather rare and unusual make-up kit came equipped with a Brownie camera and celluloid compact and rouge container in a lockable case. Also included was a lipstick and comb as the case was designed for primping before a photograph was taken. *Lori Landgrebe Antiques*. Rare.

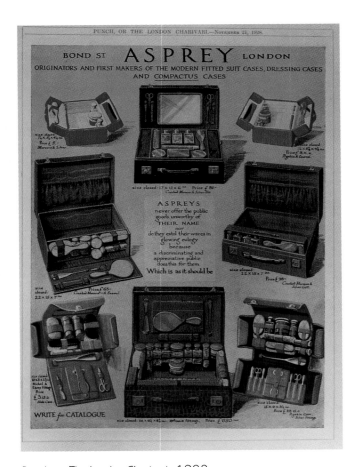

Elizabeth Arden's beauty box for the car or a vanity table. It sold for $9.00. *The Quest of The Beautiful.*

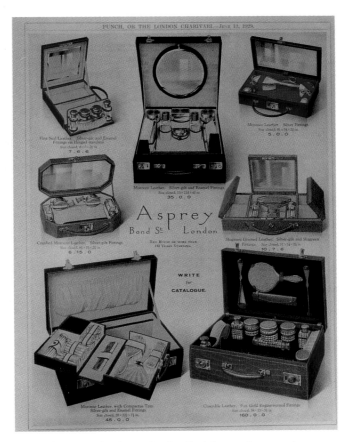

Beauty boxes and make-up kits by English manufacturer, Asprey of London, who called them dressing cases and compactus cases. *Punch, or The London Charivari*, 1929.

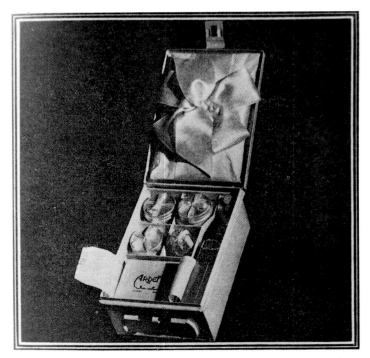

Punch, or The London Charivari, 1928.

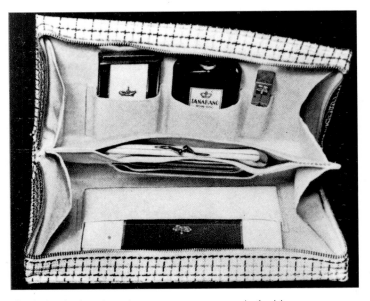

Cases for the beach enthusiast were constructed of rubber or some other hardy material and closed with a zipper which was much easier for wet hands to cope with than keys and locks. The items inside were beach appropriate. *The American Perfumer*, 1935.

Chapter Seven
Enameled & Jeweled Artistry

Most of the wonderful enameled compacts that you see today were originally created with fine jewelry store distribution in mind. Designed to enhance the appearance of an exclusive store or shop, these little gems still display fine quality workmanship and vivid colors. Fine enameled compacts were more costly and difficult to manufacture in comparison to the charming whimsical creations manufactured in bulk for the five and dime store or gift shop. High quality enameled compacts were presented in detail in the quite often colored pages of counter top catalogs and distributor directories. Enameled compact sale catalogs were used by salesclerks and at times, directories were left at the counter for the customer to leaf through when deciding on a purchase.

An example of one such exclusive shop was at the end of "Peacock Alley" in the new Waldorf Astoria Hotel which opened in October 1931. A cosmetic and beauty shop, conservative modernism struck the predominating note in this beautifully appointed and harmoniously designed salon. A glass front display case illuminated a beautiful selection of compacts, powders, and other products that could be purchased on the premises. A stairway led from the cosmetic

Charming garden scene with ladies and cat. Interestingly shaped, finely enameled with silver scrollwork border. Opens to reveal a mirror framed by gold washed border with incised decoration. Marked 800. 3¼" x 3". *From The Collection of Ann Osora.* $450-550.

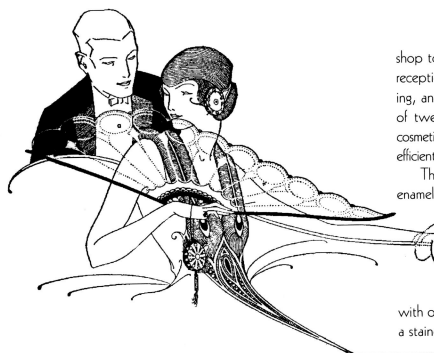

shop to the hairdressing and facial department. Beyond the reception room were the booths; twenty five for hairdressing, and five for facials. At one side of the salon was a row of twelve stationary manicure units. The entire shop, both cosmetic and salon, was appointed with the latest and most efficient equipment, beauty treatments, and products of its time.

The J.M. Fisher Company was a leader in superior quality enameled compacts. Established in the 1870s, this company produced intricately colored white metal cases often depicting detailed scenes. Some favorite subjects included parrots, fairies, boats, bathers, owls, and flying horses. Many times flowers were also depicted with other subjects, and occasionally the enameling acquired a stained glass look when multi-colored sections were used.

Artist's elaborate design drawing of a jeweled
vanity with lion's head and fish. Circa: 1910.
Courtesy of The Napier Company.

Green enameled powder compact with
intricate center, mirror, puff, powder is inside.
Pictured with a hand painted wallet. 3½" dia. *The Curiosity Shop*. $125-175.

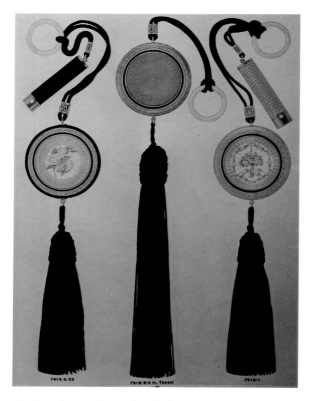

Sterling silver and enameled F&B vanities with celluloid
finger rings, mirrors, powders, and puffs along with
varying tassel sizes and lipstick options. *The Foster Blue
Book*, 1925-26.

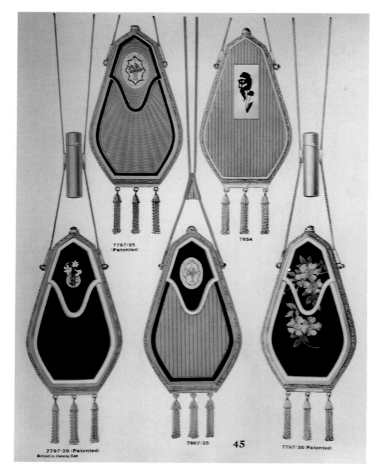

F&B enameled sterling vanities. Wholesale cost between sixty-two
to ninety dollars. *The Foster Blue Book*, 1925-26.

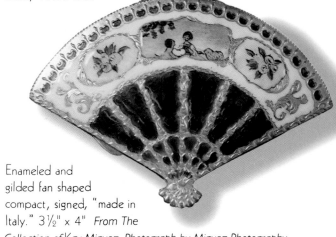

Enameled and
gilded fan shaped
compact, signed, "made in
Italy." 3½" x 4" *From The
Collection of Kay Miguez. Photograph by Miguez Photography*.

S. Kind & Sons, 1931.

F&B sterling silver powder boxes with Old English finishes. *The Foster Blue Book*, 1925-26.

Wonderful enameled compacts were originally created with fine jewelry store distribution in mind, like the Waldorf Astoria Hotel shown here in October 1931. A glass front display case illuminated a beautiful selection of compacts, powders, and other products that could be purchased on the premises. *The American Perfumer*, 1931.

The cosmetic and beauty shop at the Waldorf Astoria Hotel had stationary manicure units as well as make-up sections.

Ferd. Muelhens Inc. showroom, New York, makers of the "4711" line of toilet preparations. *The American Perfumer*.

By J.M. Fisher Company, many of these elaborate scenes came with finger rings or linked carry chains. *ACB catalog*, 1930.

The J.M. Fisher Company fancy enameled vanities. Unusual shapes with interesting titled scenes were their trademark. *ACB catalog*, 1930. $175-275.

The scenes were given simple titles such as "Fairy Pond Lilies" or "The Bather." One of the identifying characteristics of a Fisher compact is its unorthodox shape and bright colors. Fitted with a mirror, loose powder sifter, rouge, and lipstick, these treasures sold to the trade from $4.50 to $5.25 in 1930. The more expensive ones were slightly larger and included a perfume stick which now gives them an increased collectibility that embraces perfume collectors. Furnished with either a finger ring or wrist chain, the edges were usually finely etched. Fisher's slogan was "The most for the money." Today, they are highly sought after.

Along with pear shaped vanity cases and the Romantic and Oriental bolster shaped vanity purses, The Theodore W. Foster & Brothers Company manufactured many beautiful enameled compacts. Their enameling technique sometimes included pretty light colored medallions and circles of elaborate floral designs, floral baskets with ribbons and bows, cherubs, and figurals. Similar to the pear shaped vanity that finishes with three metal tassels, an octagon compact the manufacturer designed finishes with one tassel. Often, these more costly, special pieces were available with a designated shield for a monogram.

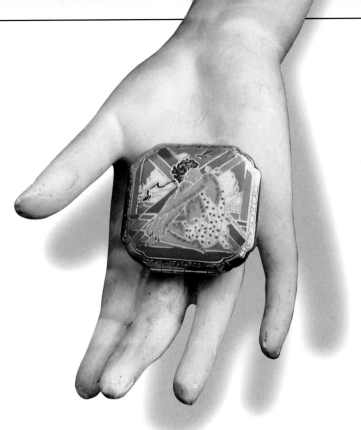

J.M. Fisher Company, bathing beauty scene with enameled painted front and white case finish. Circa: 1930. 3" x 3". *Lori Landgrebe Antiques.*

Art Deco inspired enameled on foil with silhouette of a lady on a swing under the moonlight. 3½" dia. *Lori Landgrebe Antiques.* $150-250.

Round Foster & Brothers enameled sterling compacts were attached to a matching enameled lipstick with an adjustable wrist cord or with a celluloid finger ring (made to fit like a ring on the finger with a carry cord or chain, off of which the compact dangles). The black silk tassel came in lengths varying from two to eight inches. The carry cord has gold plated filigree fittings shaped like balls. Enameling was in solid colors or with a round or oval medallion depicting flowers or birds. Ranging from sixteen to forty-three dollars, these compacts included a mirror, powder, and puff. A powder sifter was furnished for an extra fee. F & B also sold compacts without wrist chains and lipsticks that were of fine quality enamel which sold between fourteen and thirty-six dollars. Some contained powder and rouge with mirrors on the inside of the hinged cover. These compacts were usually round, sometimes oval, or octagon, and were made of fine quality sterling silver, brocaded, engine turned, enameled, Old English, and gilt finished. Old English finishing is the detailed pattern or ribbing that can be seen as part of the enameling. Florals and figurals were the main focus of enameling.

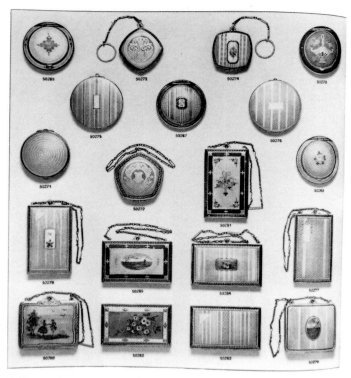

F&B powder compacts and cigarette cases. *The Foster Blue Book,* 1925-26.

Elaborate sterling silver enameled F&B vanities with metal braided carry chains and tassels. *The Foster Blue Book,* 1925-26.

Sterling F&B powder boxes, gilt finished and engine turned. The oval compact shown open reveals a powder and rouge receptacle with a lipstick container separating them. *The Foster Blue Book,* 1925-26.

F&B sterling silver powder compacts with finger rings or wrist chains. *The Foster Blue Book,* 1925-26.

Vintage Compacts & Beauty Accessories

By J.M. Fisher Company—at left is "The Ivy Vine Girls," fitted with mirror, loose powder sifter, rouge, lipstick, and perfume stick. The case is white finished with enamel painted front and a wrist chain. It sold for $5.25 in 1930, measuring 4" x 4½". In the center is the "Bathing Beauty." At right is described in early catalogs as "Japanese Scene," depicting a waterfall, which is fitted with mirror, powder sifter, rouge, and lipstick and a finger ring. It sold wholesale for $4.88 in 1930 and measures 2½" x 4". *Lori Landgrebe Antiques.* Left, $225-325; center, $175-275; right, $225-325.

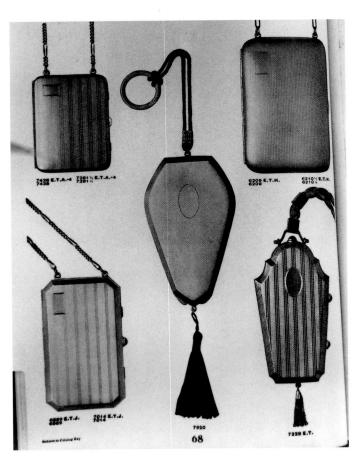

F&B fancy powder compacts. *The Foster Blue Book,* 1925-26.

Exquisitely enameled chariot scene framed by intricate gold-washed silver scrollwork. Marked 800. Shown open, interior reveals a beveled mirror framed in gold washed silver. Intricate scrollwork panel with thumb tab lifts up to access powder compartment. 3½" x 2¾". *From The Collection of Ann Osora.* Rare.

Top: enameled parrot powder compact, 3" dia. Left: Viennese enameled compact with finger ring. 3" dia. Bottom: square floral enameled powder compact. 3½" x 3½". *The Curiosity Shop*. Top, $75-125; left, $150-225; bottom, $75-125.

The Evans Company, Art Deco inspired enameled vanities. *ACB catalog*, 1930.

The Evans Company compacts with flexible handles and wrist chains. Several with Viennese enameling. *Aisenstein and Gordon catalog, 1929.*

Evans smoker set includes cigarette case, lighter, and powder compact in a French enameled front Art Deco design. Mirror, loose powder, and rouge container with finger ring attachment. The compact alone sold wholesale for $5.25, cigarette and lighter sets in presentation boxes sold for between nine and twenty-three dollars in 1930. Compact approx. 3" x 3". *Lori Landgrebe Antiques.* $150-225 set.

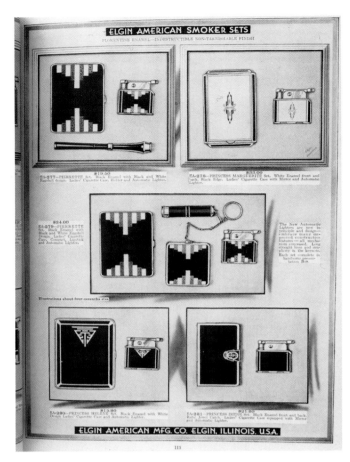

Deutsch and Marks catalog, 1932.

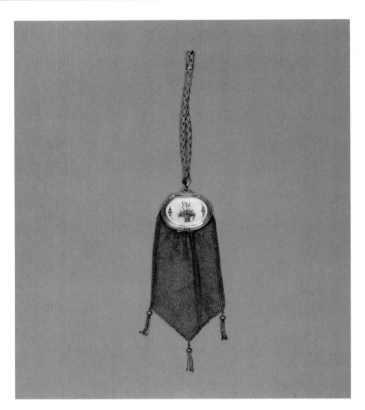

Delicately enameled vanity purse with a flower basket compact lid in sterling and a triple tasseled finished. 3" x 7". *From The Collection of Joyce Morgan, Photograph by Harry Barth. Rare.*

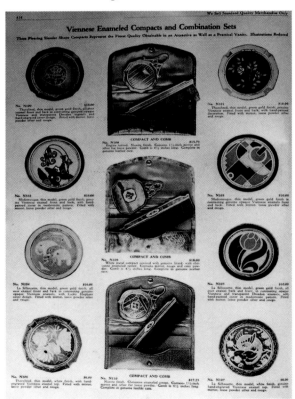

Viennese enameled compacts, some with a decided Art Deco design. *The ACB catalog, 1930.*

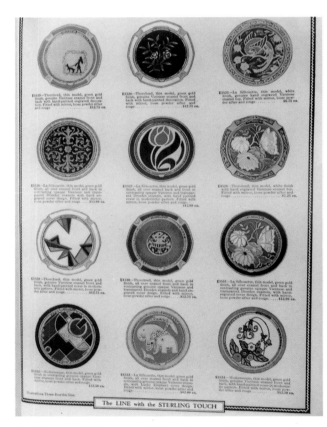

A selection of Viennese and Dresden enameled compacts. *Aisenstein and Gordon catalog, 1929.*

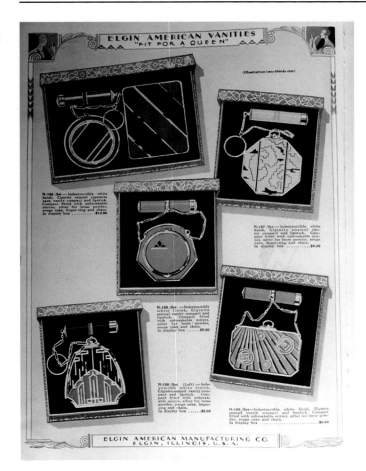

Elgin American. *ACB catalog*, 1930.

Romantic pastoral scene embellished with scrollwork, rubies, and a sapphire clasp. Interior reveals a beveled glass mirror. Marked 800. 3" x 3". *From The Collection of Ann Osora.* $400-550.

Marathon Company. Bottom left and right have lipstick tango chains attached to powder compacts. *Carson Pirie Scott and Company,* 1930.

The Foster Blue Book, 1925-26.

Rigid mesh multi-colored enameled bolster-shaped vanity purse with floral design, tassel, and carry chain. 3" x 7". *From The Collection of Joyce Morgan, Photograph by Harry Barth.* $250-300.

Left and right: two floral enameled compacts. 2½" x 3". Center: Richly embossed and enameled powder compact with finger ring chain. 3" dia. *The Curiosity Shop.* Left, $40-60; center, $75-125; right, $40-60.

R&G well made powder compact and rouge container marked "belais, 14K white gold front." Compact is heavy with an enameled carry chain that attaches to a finger ring. 3½" x 3½". *The Curiosity Shop.* $175-250.

Popular enameled compacts offered for sale in 1932.
Montgomery Ward.

Marathon Company enameled compacts, some with wrist
chains, others with finger rings called flexible handles. *Fort
Dearborn Gift Book*, 1929.

Champlevé vanity case with powder sifter, rouge, carrying chain.
Cleverly designed to hang in the shape of a diamond. 3" x 3".
Circa: 1920s. *The Curiosity Shop*. $175-200.

Elgin American. *ACB catalog*, 1930.

Artist's design drawing of a jeweled vanity. Circa: 1910. *Courtesy of The Napier Company*.

Sterling silver enameled F&B double powder boxes, a lipstick concealed in tassel was optional. *The Foster Blue Book*, 1925-26.

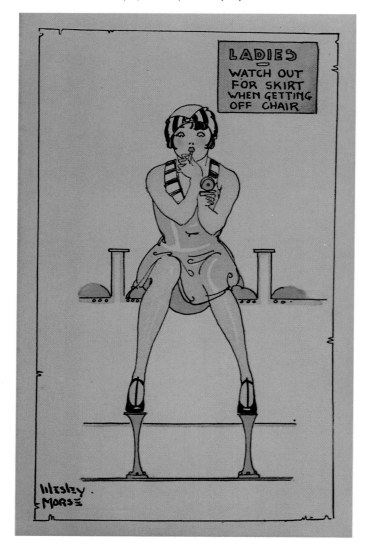

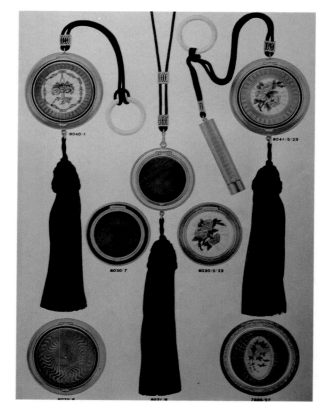

A selection of F&B enameled vanities with and without finger rings and lipsticks. *The Foster Blue Book*, 1925-26.

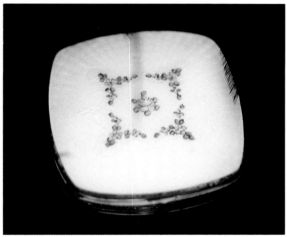

Enameled powder compact with delicate floral design.
3" x 3". *The Curiosity Shop.* $60-80.

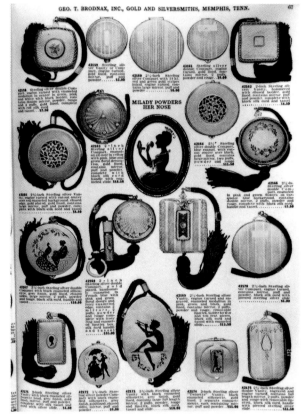

George T. Brodnax, Inc., 1926.

F&B Enameled sterling powder boxes. Finger ring chains in sterling
sold separately for $2.50. *The Foster Blue Book,* 1925-26.

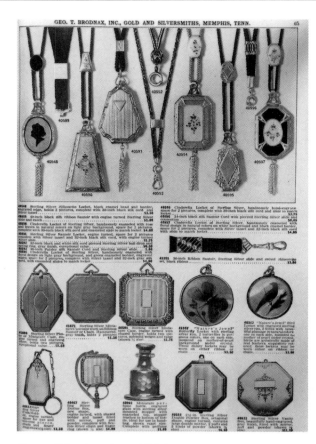

George T. Brodnax, Inc., 1926.

Enameled, silvered metal vanity case with powder, sifter, and rouge compartments, finger ring chain. Circa: 1920s. 2½" x 2½". *The Curiosity Shop.* $40-60.

Elgin American Vanities with enameling. *Fort Dearborn Gift Book,* 1929.

George T. Brodnax, Inc., 1926.

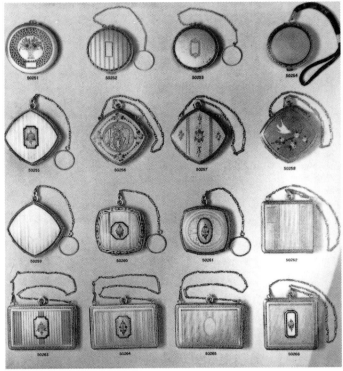

F&B silver and gold filled powder compacts. *The Foster Blue Book,* 1925-26.

Whiting and Davis jeweled and enameled vanity purse. 3½" x 7½". Author's Collection. Rare.

Enameled and Jeweled Artistry

F & B powder compacts. *The Foster Blue Book, 1925-26.*

Glass beaded compact with tassel and carry strap.
4½" dia. *From The Collection of Paula Higgins.*
$75-150.

The Evans Case Company was incorporated in 1922 in North Attleboro, Massachusetts, and was famous not only for compacts but also for cigarette lighters and other novelties. The Evans Company manufactured a nice selection of reasonably priced enameled compacts. They were sold in volume, as they were affordable for the general public.

Some of Evan's compacts had an engine turned brocade design with genuine hand engraved Viennese enamel inserts. Many were made in Art Deco designs which include colorful geometrics. Some have floral, bird, or flower basket scenes. Available with and without carry chains, finger rings and flexible handles, shapes vary to include rounds, rectangles, and squares. Most have a loose powder container, mirror, and rouge. Tango chains were also popular. These compacts ranged in wholesale price from $1.50 to $13.50.

The process of enameling had a large scope with the ability to produce an endless variety of designs and effects. One enamel could be applied on top of the other to give the appearance of flowing colors.

Enamel is a glass-like mixture of silica, quartz, borax, feldspar, and lead. Metallic oxides are added to produce the desired color. These items are ground into a fine powder and applied to the article being embellished. The enamel is then fired at a temperature of about 1700 degrees Fahrenheit so that the mixture melts and bonds to the article.

The enameling process was tricky because great care had to be given to the compact during the process. The compact had to have a higher melting point than the enameling mixture that was being applied. Compacts with more colors are most desirable since each color was fired separately. This increased the amount of time and work on the compact. Use of materials were increased, thereby making the compact more expensive. Also, there was greater risk of damage to the article being enameled. The color with the highest melting point is fired first. Those requiring progressively less heat are fired in succession. There are many types of enameling, such as cloisonné, Viennese, champlevé, basse-taille, and plique-a-jour.

For an article that was to be cloisonné, a design was drawn on the compact and traced with fine gold wire. This wire forms sections into which the enamel mixture is poured. Due to shrinkage, several firings may have been necessary to complete one color. Once all the colors are fired, the enameling is polished off, so as to become even with the top of the wires.

Champlevé is an enameling technique in which the designs are cut out from the background of the metal. The metal between these cut out areas becomes an intricate part of the design. The hollowed areas are filled with enamel and fired in succession of hardness. Once firing is complete, the compact is polished. Basse-taille designs are cut or engraved in the metal. However, instead of just filling these depressions, the entire piece is covered with a transparent enamel. Many beautiful compact designs can be achieved using this method because color varies with the depth of the design. It is easy to see that enameling helps each compact to become individual since there are color variations, however slight, in almost every one.

Plique-a-jour is an enameling method that was used to full advantage by Art Nouveau designers. It is an especially delicate method in that the enameling has no backing-only sides. To achieve this feat, the enameling mixture is used in a molasses type form. Sometimes a thin metal or mica backing is used and removed after firing. This enameling has the effect of stained glass.

Many different types of metals were used as backgrounds for enameled compacts. Copper, bronze, gold, and silver were a few. Most often, enameled compacts were sterling or silver (which has a lesser content than that of sterling), gold, or gold filled. The enameling process was executed by a specially trained individual, which required a much larger commitment for the manufacturer. It cost more and took increased production time as opposed to competitors who chose the mass produced vanity case option.

Jeweled and faux jeweled compacts are highly collectible. When the stones were genuine, they were cut by trained jewelers and the compacts sold in exclusive jewelry stores and shops. On the other hand, faux jeweled compacts were made of faceted glass stones that were imported mainly from Czechoslovakia, Austria, and Germany in the early portion of the twentieth century. These imitation gems were sold in packages by the gross. They came with foiled and unfoiled backs, depending on which the designer thought might best reflect light sources. Stones were sorted according to color and shape which included baguette, pear, round, and square.

Faux jewels were carefully set in compacts that had metal prongs, bezel settings, or empty sockets of a size to accommodate the stone. When metal prongs were used, the tiny "arms" were squeezed in around the top of the stone to hold it securely, otherwise, they were glued in the empty sockets. When the stones were bezel set, a metal band was fitted snugly around the stone to hold it in place. Such a wide variety of compact designs were created with sparkling jewels that they make a fascinating addition to any collection.

Faux jeweled and pearl vanity purse. The compact opens in the front with a tassel and carry chain, designed in the tradition of a trinity plated compact. 3¼" x 4". *From The Collection of Joyce Morgan, Photograph by Harry Barth. Rare.*

Detailed filigree faux sapphire jeweled powder and rouge compact with attached lipstick and wide finger ring. Tassel and wrist chain. 2½" dia. *Lori Landgrebe Antiques.* $275-350.

Wadsworth "Bon Bon" with prong set rhinestones. Gilded necessaire with goldtone tassel, top lid decorated with filigree leaves, blue rhinestones, and pearls. The compact top opens on a hinge to reveal mirror, sifter, and powder. The metal tassel on the bottom is used as a pull to break a vacuum-like force, allowing access to store trinkets. 1¾" x 4¾". *Author's Collection*. $200-250.

Close-up of jeweled and gilt detailed compact with thumb clasp opening. 3½" x 4". *The Curiosity Shop*. $125-175.

Elaborately jeweled vanity case set with faux pearls and jewels in gilded filigree metal. The lipstick is jeweled and rests across the bottom portion of the compact that finishes with a tassel. Shown open, the fancy jewel capped lipstick protrudes from the elaborate encasement and powder and rouge compartments can be seen on opposing sides of the compact. 4" x 4". *The Curiosity Shop*. $350-400.

Round jeweled goldtone filigree compact lid. Jewel capped tassel, carry chain. 2½" dia. Lori Landgrebe Antiques. $275-350.

Antiqued goldtone jeweled and filigree coin holder. Jeweled metal tassel, wrist chain. 1½" x 3¾". *The Curiosity Shop*. $175-225.

Bibliography

Arden, Elizabeth. *The Quest of the Beautiful.* New York.

The Andrew Jergens Company. *A Skin You Love To Touch.*

Beauty Interviews with Famous Skin Specialists. Daggett and Ramsdell, New York, New York, 1925.

The American Perfumer and Essential Oil Review. New York, 1931-1935.

Ball, Joanne Dubbs. *Costume Jewelers, The Golden Age of Design.* Schiffer Publishing, Ltd., 1990.

Basten, Fred, with Robert Salvatore and Paul A. Kaufman. *Max Factor's Hollywood.* General Publishing Group, 1995.

The Beautician. September 1926.

Carroll, Earl. *Theatre.* New York, New York, 1923.

Cosmopolitan, 1924.

Factor, Max. *Make-up by the Max Factor Method, Straight Stage Make-up.* Max Factor's Make-up Studios, Hollywood, California, 1929.

Factor, Max. *Max Factor's Hints on the Art of Make-up, Advanced Principals of Character Make-up.* Max Factor's Make-up Studios, Hollywood, California, 1930.

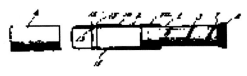

P 1,953,251

Factor, Max. *Max Factor's Hints on the Art of Make-up, Making up Youth for Older Characters.* Max Factor's Make-up Studios, Hollywood, California, 1930.

Factor, Max. *Max Factor's Hints on the Art of Make-up, Popular Stage Types.* Max Factor's Make-up Studios, Hollywood, California, 1930.

Factor, Max. *The New Art of Make-up.* Hollywood, California, 1940.

For You—Exquisite Beauty. Princess Pat, Ltd., London, England, 1932.

The Foster Blue Book. Theodore W. Foster & Brothers Company, Providence, Rhode Island, 1925, 1926.

Gerson, Roselyn. *Vintage Ladies' Compacts.* Collector Books, Paducah, Kentucky, 1996.

Harper, Martha Matilda. *Beauty Through Home Treatments.* Rochester, New York, Martha Matilda Harper, Inc., no date.

_____. *The Halo of Radiance.* Rochester, New York, Martha Matilda Harper, Inc., no date.

_____. *The Harper Method Way To Youth and Charm.* Rochester, New York, Martha Matilda Harper, Inc., 1931.

Hudnut, Richard. *Be a DuBarry Beauty.* New York, New York, no date.

_____. *Dressing Table Arts of To-day's Smart Women.* New York, Paris, no date.

The Jewelers' Circular. 1920.

Judge. New York, New York, 1921, 1922.

The Ladies Home Journal. 1922, 1924, 1928, 1929, 1931.

Modern Make-up by Stein, Half Century of Progress in Theatrical Make-up. M. Stein Cosmetic Company, New York, New York, 1936.

Mueller, Laura M. *Collector's Encyclopedia of Compacts, Carryalls & Face Powder Boxes*. Collector Books, Paducah, Kentucky, 1994.

The New Yorker. 1928.

The Pictorial Review. August 1918, 1919.

Punch or The London Charivari. London, England, 1928, 1929.

The Saturday Evening Post. 1922.

Schwartz, Lynell K. *Vintage Purses at Their Best*. Schiffer Publishing, Ltd., Atglen, Pennsylvania, 1995.

Thorn, Rose. *Beauty Secrets*. Berkeley, California, 1919.

_____. *What Every Woman Should Know*. Berkeley, California, Rose Thorn Company, Circa 1919.

Vogue. 1950.

Index

About the Author

Proprietor of *The Curiosity Shop*, located in Cheshire, Connecticut, Lynell Schwartz is an antique dealer who exhibits at leading antique shows in New York, New Jersey, Connecticut, and Massachusetts. She manages estate sales, and carries a diversified range of antiques, specializing in the buying and selling of fine antique purses, purse frames, ladies' compacts, costume jewelry, and ladies' accessories. She also operates a mail order business and produces a color catalog of items for sale. Her antiques have been photographed for national magazines and newspapers. She is a member of *The Compact Collector's Club* and *The Vintage Fashion Jewelry Club*.

She studied journalism and wrote *Vintage Purses at Their Best*, published by Schiffer Publishing, Ltd. in 1995. She has also written vintage fashion articles published by *Lady's Gallery Magazine*.

The Curiosity Shop
P.O. Box 964
Cheshire, CT 06410

Your comments, ideas, or questions, along with an SASE for a response, are welcome and can be sent to the above address.

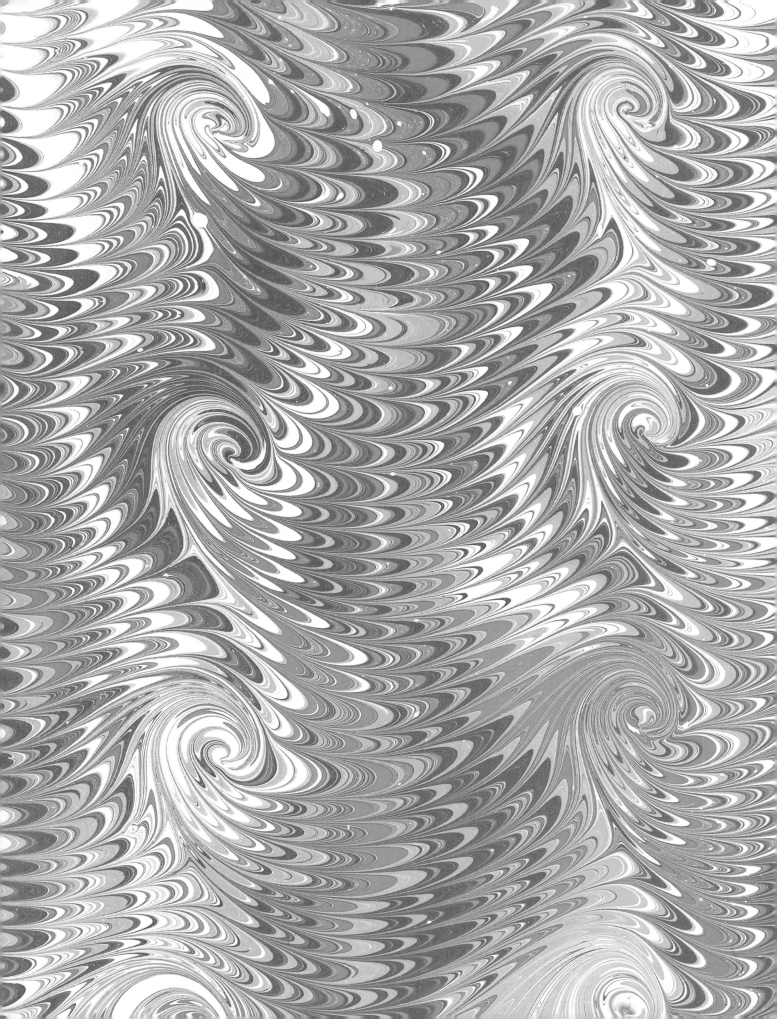